SECRETS O

Secrets of
New Babylon

LEFT BEHIND
>THE KIDS<

Jerry B. Jenkins

Tim LaHaye

WITH CHRIS FABRY

TYNDALE HOUSE PUBLISHERS, INC.
WHEATON, ILLINOIS

Visit Tyndale's exciting Web site at www.tyndale.com

Discover the latest Left Behind news at www.leftbehind.com

Published in association with the literary agency of Alive Communications, Inc., 7680 Goddard Street, Suite 200, Colorado Springs, CO 80920.

Edited by Curtis H. C. Lundgren

ISBN 0-8423-4315-6, mass paper

Printed in the United States of America

08 07 06 05 04 03 02
9   8   7   6   5   4   3   2   1

To Patrick Hagen

TABLE OF CONTENTS

What's Gone On Before

THE Young Tribulation Force is involved in an incredible adventure. The kids have witnessed global vanishings and a worldwide earthquake. Now demon locusts have covered the earth.

As Judd Thompson Jr. arrives in Israel, he finds Lionel Washington and their new friend, Sam Goldberg. When they try to talk with Sam's father at a Jerusalem hospital, the kids narrowly escape Global Community guards.

Vicki Byrne and the others staying at the schoolhouse try desperately to help the unbelievers, but Melinda and Janie are stung by the locusts. Mysteriously, Charlie is not bitten.

Mark Eisman returns to the schoolhouse with a new member of the Young Tribulation Force, Carl Meninger. Vicki agrees to travel south to warn and teach the underground church. When the kids receive a message about believers in danger to the north, they set out to alert them.

While Judd discusses his future with a young woman named Nada, he receives a plea from Pavel, his friend in New Babylon. Judd agrees to visit. While traveling, Judd learns Pavel is dying from a disease. Then, to his horror, he discovers Nada has stowed away in the plane.

Vicki and the others find a group of believers in Johnson City, Tennessee. She tries to warn them of the GC threat, but some won't believe her.

Join the kids as they struggle to elude the Global Community and tell others the truth.

ONE

The Rescue

VICKI Byrne heard rumbling outside the bowling alley and desperately wanted to make a break for the motorcycle. But she couldn't run. At least a hundred people inside needed her help.

She and Conrad had seen Global Community guards nearby. Demon locusts buzzed around the specially equipped vans. The guards inside wore protective clothing.

People whimpered and cried as the pastor tried to calm them. "No matter what happens, we trust in the Lord!"

Conrad ran to the front of the building. "I don't see anything in the parking lot!"

"They must be around back!" someone shouted.

Vicki took the microphone and explained what the kids had heard from Carl Meninger, their friend working as a Global Community Peacekeeper. "The GC has discovered where believers are meeting. They want to make examples of us and a group in Maryland."

"Are they going to kill us?" a woman said.

"We don't know," Vicki said, "but we have to get out of here."

Someone banged on a metal door in the back.

Conrad shouted, "The white vans are still on the hill."

"Then who's at the door?" Vicki said.

Someone shouted and pounded on the door again. Vicki thought she recognized the voice.

❋

Judd Thompson Jr. couldn't believe his eyes. Lionel Washington and Sam Goldberg stood by an empty box in the airplane. Beside it stood his friend Nada.

"How did you get here?" Judd said.

Nada stared at him. "Aren't you happy to see me?"

Judd glanced at Lionel and Sam. "Of course, but—"

"I stowed away in a box of pamphlets," Nada said. "I wanted to be with you when you meet your friend in New Babylon." Nada explained how she emptied a box of pamphlets and marked it "Main Cabin."

The plane dipped and lightning flashed. The pilot, Mac McCullum, spoke through the intercom. "Better buckle up and hang on."

Nada sat by Judd. "You look angry."

"I'm not! I'm just concerned. You've put us in a bad situation."

"How?"

"This is Nicolae Carpathia's plane. We were only cleared for three people in New Babylon. When four of us get off, we could be in trouble. Or we could put Mac in a tight spot."

Judd explained what Mac had said about Judd's friend Pavel. Their visit had been cleared because "it's his last wish that I visit him."

"Pavel is dying?" Nada said.

Judd nodded.

"What's going to happen when we get there?"

The plane dropped suddenly and Judd felt his stomach surge.

"Sorry about that," Mac said on the intercom. "This is a rough one. Stay in your seats."

"I have to talk with you," Judd said.

Mac came on the intercom. "Wait till we get out of these clouds, Judd."

Judd looked at Nada. Could Mac hear everything they were saying? Could he also hear Nicolae Carpathia when he was on the plane?

"I'll let you know when it's safe," Mac said.

Lightning flashed again. Nada whispered something.

"What did you say?" Judd said.

Nada turned. Her eyes were red. "There's another reason I had to come with you."

"What?" Judd said.

Nada put a hand to her forehead. "I can't go home. I'm running away."

※

Vicki ran to the back door. Conrad and the pastor told her to stop, but she ignored them. The door wouldn't open.

"What are you doing?" Conrad shouted.

"Hang on!" Vicki said, finally opening the door.

Sunshine poured in and Vicki saw her friend Shelly. Behind her was Pete's huge truck and trailer. Pete ran to meet them.

"The GC are on the hill behind us," Vicki said.

"I saw 'em when I drove in," Pete said. "How many people you got in here?"

Vicki showed him, then started to introduce the pastor. Pete cut her off. "No time to chat. That guy back at the gas station, Roger, told me on the radio that there's a couple of huge transport vehicles headed our way."

"They're going to arrest us?" the pastor said.

"Not if I can help it," Pete said. "I'll back the truck up as close as I can to the door and you get the people in a single file. If we work fast, we can get everybody in without them knowing what's going on."

Conrad raced up. "The vans are pulling out. Coming our way."

※

"Nada!" Judd said. "You can't run away from your family!"

"To be with you," Nada said, "I have to."

"Wait. Back up. Start from the beginning."

Nada took a deep breath. "I told my mother you and I were getting more serious. She was excited for me. She likes you a lot. But . . ."

"Your father?"

Nada looked away. "She said he likes you as a person but doesn't think we should go further with our relationship."

Judd frowned. "He's entitled to his opin-ion."

"But he said if you return to Israel, we can't be together. I was afraid I'd never see you again."

Judd pulled Nada's head to his shoulder and brushed her hair with a hand. "You should call your folks and tell them—"

"No!" Nada said, jerking away. "They'll make me come back."

"They'll blame me," Judd said. "Neither of us wants that."

Nada stared at Judd. "You're scared of him! You care more about what my father thinks than you do about me."

Judd shook his head. "I just want to do this the right way. Your dad changed his mind once about me. When he sees how much I care about you, he'll change it again."

"You don't know my father," she said. "He can be so stubborn."

Judd smiled. "A family trait?"

Nada opened her mouth wide and punched Judd in the shoulder.

❋

Vicki helped people onto the truck. Pete told them to move to the front and sit in tight rows. Some panicked and pushed their way inside.

"Where are you taking us?" an older man said.

"Away from the GC," Pete said.

Locusts buzzed at the back door but apparently flew away when they realized the occupants were believers.

Conrad returned. "Can't see the vans. Probably take them five minutes to get past the ridge."

Vicki nodded. As people hurried past she said, "Stay calm." She noticed a woman with a small electronic device. "What's that?"

"I record the meetings," the woman said. "I play it for people who can't get here."

"Can I have it?" Vicki said.

"But—"

"Trust me," Vicki said.

The woman handed over the recording and Vicki raced to the office and put it into the machine. A man's voice came through the speakers. "Before we get started, we want to let anyone who wants lead us in prayer."

"Perfect," Vicki said. She turned up the speakers full blast and found the switch for speakers outside the bowling alley.

When she reached the back door, Pete was closing the truck. "Let's get out of here."

Once the plane made it through the storm, Judd headed to the cockpit.

"How were you able to hear us?" Judd said.

Mac stared at him. "Can't tell you. Let's just say the conversations back there are relayed to the rest of the Tribulation Force."

Judd explained the situation with Nada.

"The GC let you come because of Pavel's condition," Mac said. "Carpathia has no idea the cargo hold is jammed with Ben-Judah's studies in different languages. An extra person is gonna raise a red flag."

"Why do they have to know?"

"Cargo's one thing," Mac said. "Human beings are another. If the guards notice Nada, we could be in trouble."

Judd scratched his head.

Mac said, "What kind of ID does she have?"

Judd went back and got it from Nada, then showed it to Mac. "Her brother was with the GC in New Babylon. Killed in the earth-quake."

"You serious?" Mac said.

"He was a Peacekeeper in Carpathia's main complex."

Mac flipped a few switches and pulled out

his cell phone. "What was her brother's name?"

Judd told him and returned to his seat.

A few minutes later, Mac called Judd and Nada forward. "I got through to one of my superiors, one of the few who hasn't been stung yet. I told him I'd located a family member of a deceased GC worker who wanted to pay her respects. They're putting you up in the main complex. Who knows, you might even get to meet Carpathia himself."

Vicki sat next to Pete as he pulled the truck out of the parking lot.

"So far so good," he said as they chugged onto the road back to town.

"What about all the cars in the parking lot?" Vicki said.

"I bet the GC will hang around and wait for people to come back."

"And then nab them," Vicki said. "Guess we just lost our motorcycle."

Pete gave a low whistle. "Up ahead."

Coming around a curve in the distance were the two vans, colored lights swirling on top. Between them was a huge bus with the Global Community insignia on the side.

"Stay calm," Pete said.

The first van passed going far over the speed limit. The wind from the bus nearly drove Pete off the road. The second van slowed and blocked the truck.

"Let me handle this," Pete said.

"I should warn the others," Vicki said. "Some of us could get away."

Pete put a hand on her shoulder.

A GC Peacekeeper stepped out of the van and was swarmed by locusts. The man slapped them away from his white protective suit and motioned for Pete to roll down his window.

Pete didn't seem nervous. "What can I do for you?"

"You just came from that bowling alley back there."

"Me and my little sister got sidetracked. Had to turn around."

"Where you headed?"

"Got a delivery in town," Pete said. "Hope we make it before the load goes bad."

The man moved back, swatting at locusts. "What kind of load—"

"Sure was a wacky bunch back there," Vicki interrupted. Pete gave her a look.

"What do you mean?" the man said.

"I heard all this preaching and hollering,"

Vicki said. "You need to put those people away before they hurt somebody."

The Peacekeeper looked toward the bowling alley. Vicki noticed through her outside mirror that the other van and the bus had reached the parking lot. Several officers in protective gear pointed guns toward the building.

A radio squawked from the other van. "They're here! We need backup!"

The Peacekeeper rushed back to his van and sped away.

"Good work," Pete said.

"Thanks," Vicki said. "Wonder how long it'll take them to figure out it's not a real meeting?"

"Hopefully long enough to get these people to safety."

Pete took the curves at full speed and Vicki wondered how those in the back were holding on.

"Up there!" Vicki shouted, pointing. The ramp to the highway rose in the distance. She jumped in her seat. "We've made it!"

Pete put up a hand and shook his head. A siren wailed behind them. Vicki's heart sank as she checked the mirror.

TWO

The Peacekeepers' Mistake

"FLOOR it!" Vicki shouted.

Pete shook his head. "No way. They'll know we're up to something." He pulled to the side of the road and bowed his head. "Lord, protect us." The siren wailed behind them. "And please do it fast. Amen."

Pete opened the door and jumped down. Vicki followed close. The GC van skidded to a stop in the middle of the road and a man shouted, "Stop where you are, hands in the air!"

They both put their hands over their heads. "Something wrong?" Pete shouted.

A Peacekeeper stepped out, surrounded by locusts. He smacked at them with his gun and pointed at Vicki. "On the ground! Hands on your head."

Vicki sat in the road. The Peacekeeper trained the gun on Pete.

"What did we do?" Pete said.

Vicki studied the guard's protective white suit. On his back was an oxygen generator. A series of heavy-duty zippers connected the boots with the rest of the suit. The helmet was made of shiny plastic and latched into the collar. Locusts pinged off the face shield and swarmed near the man's legs. "Apollyon!" they screamed, but they couldn't get through.

"We counted more than a hundred people going into that bowling alley," the Peacekeeper said.

"Bowling can take your mind off your problems," Pete said.

The Peacekeeper didn't smile. "Now the place is empty. A tape was playing."

"That's what I heard?" Vicki said.

"Shut up! Open the truck!" The Peacekeeper waved toward the van and the other man, short and round, got out. The suit made him look like a snowman. He pointed his gun at Pete. A small red dot appeared on Pete's chest.

At the back of the man's protective gear Vicki noticed a zipper at the bottom of the heel. Pete frowned and walked to the trailer.

"Open it now!"

Pete unlatched the door and grabbed the handle. Just as he was about to swing it open, Vicki reached and quickly unzipped Snowman's heel. A locust immediately moved into the hole and began chewing at the inner lining, a thin layer of plastic.

Vicki scooted left and unzipped the other Peacekeeper's suit. Several locusts moved in, their hideous voices screaming.

Pete opened both doors, revealing the huddled mass of believers. Conrad and Shelly, near the door, squinted at the light.

An alarm sounded in Snowman's helmet. He cursed as air hissed from his leg. "Oxygen breach!"

"Your leg!" the other yelled.

The man screamed, dropped his gun, and fell in a heap.

The other Peacekeeper ran toward him as an alarm sounded in his suit. He stopped and swatted at the locusts boring through the plastic at his heel. Before he could zip his suit, he straightened, threw his arms into the air, and let out a terrifying scream. He pitched forward and smashed face first onto the pavement. Locusts swarmed.

Pete ran to the GC van, grabbed the keys, and threw them over an embankment. Vicki did the same with the guns.

"Let's get out of here," Pete said, taking something from the van.

"What about them?" Vicki said. One guard writhed, the other lay still, unconscious.

"It's already too late for them," Pete said.

❋

Judd told Lionel and Sam what was going on as the plane neared New Babylon. At Mac's suggestion, Nada took his cell phone and called her parents in Israel.

Judd returned to the cockpit. He guessed Mac was about fifty. Mac said he was twice divorced, no kids. He had flown commercial and military planes.

"How did you become a member of the Tribulation Force?" Judd said.

"It's a long story, but briefly, I was flying with a guy who had become a believer after his wife and son disappeared. He told me his story and I believed. When I went to tell him, I saw the mark on his forehead. That was some morning."

"Where were you when the earthquake hit?"

"Right on top of Carpathia's building," Mac said. "Makes me sick to think about it. The guy actually kicked people away from the helicopter so he could save his own skin."

"So Nada's brother didn't have a chance," Judd said.

"The only ones with a prayer were the people on the roof. If her brother was inside or nearby, he was probably killed instantly. Leon Fortunato says he himself was killed in the collapse."

"Yeah, he says Carpathia raised him from the dead."

Mac snickered. "I say Leon's as big a liar as Nicolae."

He pointed out New Babylon on the horizon and a strange feeling came over Judd. It was as if they were entering a place of evil. Judd had heard and read so much about the gleaming buildings and streets second to none. After the earthquake, Nicolae Carpathia had made rebuilding the city his top priority.

As the plane neared the city, Judd was impressed by the sparkle of glass in the sunshine. Beautiful buildings rose out of the sand, each a monument celebrating the reign of Nicolae Carpathia.

Judd went back to his seat. Nada was wiping her eyes.

"What happened?" Judd said.

Nada laid her head on his shoulder. "They were frantic trying to find me. Yitzhak and my father had just gotten back from looking in the streets."

"What did you tell them?"

"That I didn't mean to cause trouble. I just wanted to be with you. I told my mother I was going to visit the place where Kasim died."

"Let me guess. It didn't help."

"No. And my father was so angry he could hardly talk. I told him I loved him and would see him soon. He called me an impulsive teenager." She imitated her father's voice, " 'We don't have time to play love games. A wrong move could cost our lives.' "

Nada's father was right. She was impulsive. But that appealed to Judd.

Mac landed and escorted the kids through a private entrance for GC employees. He explained that the believers working behind the scenes for the Global Community had faked locust stings.

"Are there many believers here?" Lionel said.

"Not many," Mac said, "but we're finding new ones who read Tsion Ben-Judah's Web site. We have a guy who knows computers. There's another pilot. And we hope many more new believers before we have to get out of here."

"Why wouldn't you stay?" Lionel said.

"Sooner or later Carpathia will make everybody take some form of ID right on their skin. You'll have to have it to buy or sell or move around."

Mac told Nada to be careful. "If anyone finds out you're a believer, they'll report you in a second."

"Just keep quiet and let them go to hell?" Nada said.

Mac scratched his neck. "If you were my kids, I'd say the same thing."

Judd and the others nodded.

"How do we get back home?" Nada said.

Mac shrugged. "I doubt you'll be able to fly commercial. Let Judd work that out with this Pavel and his dad."

Mac led them through the nearly deserted airport. The locusts had hit the GC hard. An older man checked the kids' identification. Mac explained who they were, and the man eyed them carefully, then waved them through.

※

Vicki held on as Pete drove as fast as possible to the highway. She kept watching for the white GC vans.

Pete pulled out a tiny radio and flipped it on. "I got it from the van."

The radio squawked message after message to the downed Peacekeepers. Finally, another crew reported the mishap.

"They'll come after us now," Pete said.

He took an exit and barreled into the gas station where he had switched trailers. Pete raced inside. Vicki opened the trailer and the people tumbled out, looking dazed and disoriented.

"We thought we were goners," Shelly said.

A call came over the radio. "We're almost to the highway. They couldn't have gotten far."

Pete returned with Roger Cornwell and yelled for everyone to be quiet. "They're on their way, so we have to hide. I'm taking the truck back to the highway—"

"No!" Vicki shouted.

"It's the only way," Pete said. "Roger says there's a cave about a half a mile back in the trees behind the station."

"We know where it is," a teenage boy shouted.

"Good," Pete said. "Lead the way."

"But, Pete," Vicki pleaded.

"Trust me," Pete said. "I'll be all right."

Vicki ran with the others into the woods.

She stopped at the tree line and watched Pete drive away. "Protect him," she prayed.

※

New Babylon gleamed in the sunlight. Mac drove near all the sights the kids had seen on television and pointed out significant buildings and landmarks. The streets were nearly deserted. Locusts were out in full force, waiting to sting anyone without the mark of the believer.

When they came to Nicolae Carpathia's office complex, Mac slowed. He told them the structure had been built on the same site as the old building that had collapsed during the great earthquake.

"This is where my brother worked," Nada said, her voice trembling.

"You'll stay in the apartment complex over there," Mac said.

"What about us?" Lionel said.

Mac stopped and opened the door for Nada. "You guys are down a few more blocks."

Judd hugged Nada. "Be careful," he said. "I want us back in Israel in one piece."

Nada smiled. "You're the one I'm worried about."

Out of the corner of his eye, Judd saw Lionel shake his head.

THREE

Charlie's Breakthrough

MARK Eisman struggled with his role at the schoolhouse. He wanted to follow the latest news and work on their Web site, www.theunderground-online.com, but with Vicki, Conrad, and Shelly gone, and no chance of Judd or Lionel returning soon, his job was holding everything together.

Lenore Barker was a big help with the daily chores, but she had to look after her baby, Tolan. Melinda and Janie, who had been stung by locusts, suffered great pain. They wailed and moaned from their room upstairs.

Mark put Darrion Stahley in charge of following the travels of Vicki and the others. She had kept in contact with the kids through South Carolina, but something went wrong as they neared Tennessee. Darrion hadn't heard anything more from them. She also monitored what was going on in Baltimore with another crackdown on believers. She kept track of incoming e-mail and watched for news from Carl Meninger at the GC outpost in Florida.

But Mark was baffled by Charlie. He was the only unbeliever who hadn't been stung. Lenore and Darrion met with Mark after dinner to talk.

"I don't know what to think," Darrion said. "If he were disabled in some way he would have been taken in the Rapture, right?"

"There must be some way to explain it," Mark said.

Lenore shook her head. "If it hadn't been for you guys, I wouldn't have escaped those things."

"Let me throw something out," Mark said. "The locusts didn't sting Tolan because he's a baby. Even though he doesn't have the mark on his forehead, God must have put some kind of protection around him."

"OK," Darrion said.

"What if there's some kind of protection from God around Charlie?"

"But he's had every chance in the world," Darrion said. "From what Vicki said, he wants to be part of the club. He's still trying to do things to earn the mark."

Mark nodded. "But maybe he's so close

that . . ." He noticed someone at the kitchen door.

"I've been trying to figure it out myself," Charlie said, walking inside. He sat slowly, a strange look on his face. "I know I deserve to get stung just like those two girls, but I didn't."

"Charlie, you've heard what Vicki and the rest of us have said about God," Darrion said. "You know the truth, right?"

"I know that if I want to get a thing on my head, I have to pray that prayer."

"Is that why you prayed?" Mark said.

Charlie looked away. "Vicki was nice to me. I wanted to be one of you guys. Nobody's ever liked me because I'm kind of weird. And I know God doesn't like me."

"Wait," Mark said, "the whole point is that God loves you. He cares about you."

"He likes you if you do good things," Charlie argued.

Mark moved closer. "We were just wondering if maybe God protected you because he knew you were close to really understanding and accepting his love."

Charlie wrinkled his brow. "Why would he do that?"

"God loved you enough to die for you," Darrion said. "Protecting you from those locusts is nothing compared to that."

Charlie closed his eyes.

Mark looked at Darrion and Lenore and whispered, "Pray."

***

Judd said good-bye to Mac and thanked him. "We'd never have made it here without you."

"Be careful," Mac said, "these buildings have ears. Call me if you need anything."

The kids made their way through a series of doors designed to keep the locusts out. They found the elevators and Judd punched the right floor number. The building had an atrium with exotic flowers, plants, and a huge waterfall. The only thing missing was people. Judd figured they were either cocooned in their rooms or recuperating from their stings.

"I wouldn't mind living like this," Sam said.

"I'd rather live in a tent than work for Nicolae Carpathia," Lionel said.

Judd put a finger to his lips. "Remember what Mac said about this place having ears?"

The three got off the elevator and looked for Pavel's apartment. A door opened and a man in uniform stepped out, a hat pulled low across his face. "What are you doing out without proper protection?"

"We're looking for a friend," Judd said. "His name is Pavel."

The man smiled and took off his hat. Judd sighed when he saw the mark of the true believer on his forehead.

"You must be Judd," the man said, extending his hand. "I'm Pavel's father, Anton Rudja."

Judd introduced Lionel and Sam and they went inside. "Why didn't Pavel tell me about his illness?" Judd said.

"You weren't supposed to know," Mr. Rudja said. "Pavel has the idea that he is going to be healed."

"What's wrong with him?" Lionel said.

Mr. Rudja whispered, "The doctors aren't sure. The disease weakens his muscles and bone structure. There are other diseases like it, but nothing quite like what he's going through."

"Is he able to see us?" Judd said.

Mr. Rudja smiled. "When he can speak, it is all he talks about. He has to stay in bed almost all day now."

Mr. Rudja explained how he had gained clearance from the Global Community for them to come to New Babylon. "My superior knows about Pavel and I told him he wanted his friend from the North American States to visit. Since he may not have much time . . ." Mr. Rudja looked away and shook his head.

"I'm sorry. I promised him I would not be emotional about this."

"We understand," Judd said.

Lionel and Sam waited in the living room while Judd met with Pavel. The shades were drawn and the room was dark. Judd let his eyes focus and recognized the pictures on the wall and the furniture in the room. This was what he had seen every time Pavel hooked up with him via computer.

The boy slept, his head propped up with pillows. A piece of medical equipment stood like a soldier by the bed. It beeped every few seconds and lights blinked. Judd took the boy's hand. No response. He knelt by the bed, still holding Pavel's hand, and prayed.

"God, I thank you that you brought Pavel to yourself and that you used him to help his father know the truth. Please heal him and make him well. In Jesus' name. Amen."

Pavel squeezed Judd's hand weakly and smiled. "You made it."

"Why didn't you tell me how sick you are?" Judd said.

"Would it have changed anything?" Pavel said. "You are my friend. I knew you would come."

"You're right," Judd said.

"I have good news," Pavel said. "God is healing me."

✳

Vicki ran behind the others thinking about the danger Pete was in. The GC would surely catch him. What then? Would they throw him in prison?

The pastor of the group worked his way back and helped Vicki. "Watch your step as we go up the side of the mountain."

The dirt path wound through trees and seemed to go straight up. People huffed and puffed as they climbed over rocks. Vicki was the last to make it to the top. The mouth of the cave could fit two people; then the passage opened into a huge cavern. Burnt wood lay in piles throughout the cave.

"This was our meeting place after the earthquake," the pastor said. "The bowling alley was more convenient for everyone so we moved there."

Shelly rushed back to Vicki, trembling. "I told them I didn't like caves. Last time I was in one of these—"

Vicki put a hand on Shelly's shoulder. "I know, the snakes. You're going to be OK."

The pastor called people together and prayed for Pete. Another prayed for Roger at the gas station.

Conrad whispered to Vicki, "The kid who

led us up here says everybody's desperate for more teaching."

Vicki frowned. "There's no way I'm going to get up in front of all these people."

"You did it in South Carolina," Shelly said.

"But there weren't that many," Vicki said.

"I told the pastor what you know," Conrad said.

"You what?"

Before Conrad could respond the pastor said, "You all know how new to this I am. Well, we have someone with us who wants to encourage us." He motioned to Vicki. Vicki looked around the crowded cave.

"Come on, girl," someone said.

People clapped and the pastor called for quiet. "We don't need to make the GC's job any easier." He turned to Vicki. "The floor's yours, young lady."

※

Mark tried to talk with Charlie, but the boy ran from the schoolhouse.

"You want me to go get him?" Darrion said.

Lenore said, "I think that boy is starting to understand. Leave him alone."

An hour later, Mark found Charlie on the hillside near the grave of the other Morale

Monitor, Felicia. His eyes were red. "I drank some of that poison water but I didn't die. That bug thing flew near me but turned around and stung Melinda. Why?"

"I don't know," Mark said, "but I think it has something to do with God loving you."

"What do you mean?"

"God wants you to be his child. He cares what happens to you."

"I want to be his son," Charlie said. "Before, I just wanted to be one of you guys."

"In the Gospel of John it says that if you believe in him and accept him, he gives you the right to become a child of God."

"That's what I've been trying to do," Charlie said. "I've tried really hard to do what's right so God and you guys would accept me."

Mark got down on one knee. "That's where you've made the mistake. You don't do anything to get God to accept you. If you believe you've done bad things and ask God to forgive you, he'll come into your life and change you."

Charlie opened his eyes wide. "So he'll help me do things the way he wants me to do them?"

"Yes."

"You're saying if I want to be a child of God, I don't have to do good stuff, I just believe that Jesus is God and ask him to change me?"

Mark nodded. "You want me to pray with you?"

Charlie shook his head. "No, I want to do this myself." He closed his eyes. "God, I think I understand. Thank you for protecting me from those bugs and that poison water. I don't just want that thing on my forehead. I want to be your kid.

"Forgive me for the bad stuff I've done. I believe you died for me and I believe you came alive again like Vicki said. Help me to do what you want me to do from now on. Amen."

Mark smiled. Charlie looked around the hillside and took a deep breath. He turned to Mark. "I see it! On your forehead! It looks like a cross, doesn't it?"

Charlie ran to the schoolhouse and found Lenore, then Darrion. Mark couldn't wait to talk with Vicki and tell her the news.

※

Vicki felt nervous as she spoke, but the more she saw how eager people were, the more she relaxed. She explained how she had become a believer and what Pastor Bruce Barnes had taught her. "He showed us the truth of the

Bible and he lived it in front of us. He even adopted me before he died."

Vicki paused to compose herself. A few people whispered prayers. "I studied the Bible on my own and with friends, but I figured no one could ever take the place of Bruce. But not long after we lost Pastor Barnes, I met Tsion Ben-Judah."

Someone gasped. "You actually met him?"

Vicki nodded. "And the things I learned from reading his messages and hearing him speak have changed my life. This gathering here is evidence that what he's saying is true. We're in the midst of a great soul harvest when millions will come to know God personally."

A young man raised a hand. "What's going to happen next?"

Vicki took a deep breath. She didn't want to scare the people, but she knew the truth wouldn't be easy to take.

FOUR

Vicki's Prediction

JUDD introduced Lionel and Sam to Pavel.

Pavel was interested in Sam's situation. "I know what it's like to have a father who doesn't believe. Don't give up."

The conversation turned to Nicolae Carpathia. Pavel glanced at a clock and said, "The television transmission I told you about is supposed to begin in about twenty minutes."

"Where is Carpathia?" Lionel said.

"From what I've heard, he and his right-hand man, Leon Fortunato, are holed up in an underground bunker that keeps out the locusts."

"Any idea how many top GC people have been stung?" Sam said.

"The ten kings, or rulers as Nicolae calls them, have all been stung. So has Peter the Second."

"Serves him right," Judd muttered.

"The GC news would never report this, but my father said two of Peter the Second's staff were executed before the locusts came."

Lionel gasped. "Executed? What happened?"

"They repeated something they heard in Peter's office. Peter said the information was private and had them shot."

Lionel shook his head. "Just what you want in a religious leader."

"This will really make you sick," Pavel said. "Nicolae sent Peter a note of congratulations."

Judd sighed. "What do you expect from the most evil man on the planet?"

"The word's out that Christian literature is everywhere," Pavel said, "but no one knows how it's being transported."

"For Mac's sake, let's hope it stays that way," Judd said.

"My father also said that there's talk of requiring everyone to worship Nicolae. I hope I never live to see that. . . ." Pavel paused, realizing what he had just said.

"Come on," Judd said, "let's watch old Nicolae make a fool of himself."

The kids gathered around to watch the live broadcast. Television producers had tried to spruce up the fallout shelter, putting up backdrops and arranging furniture. Nicolae appeared to be sitting in his office, the skyline of New Babylon behind him. But there was something strange about his voice.

"Sounds boomy," Lionel said, "like he's broadcasting from my basement."

"Ladies and gentlemen of the Global Community, I bring you greetings from the greatest city on the face of the earth, New Babylon."

Nicolae turned as if he were looking out the window. As Carpathia continued, a locust flew onto his shoulder and landed. Judd moved closer to the TV to get a better look.

Nicolae gave several statistics about the positive things that had happened since he had taken over the world system. He assured viewers he was in control. Suddenly he stopped, as if he had just seen the locust on his shoulder. The locust leaned toward Nicolae's ear.

Nicolae smiled. "Yes, I know we have heard reports about poisonous bites coming from these harmless creatures. While there may be some truth to those rumors, rest assured they are exaggerated."

"It's a trick," Judd said. "That locust isn't real; it's computer generated."

Nicolae turned to the locust. "Do you

think a cute little fellow like this would harm anyone? Of course not. I urge all the followers of the Global Community to put aside fear. While these beings are new to our world, there is no reason to panic or hide."

"And he's saying this from an underground bunker," Lionel said.

"In order to ease fears about the world economy," Nicolae continued, "I am personally taking charge of global commerce."

"What does that mean?" Sam said.

Pavel coughed and lay back on a pillow. "It means he can pay off his ten kings and keep them loyal."

Carpathia put up a hand to pet the locust. The camera zoomed in on his face. Judd thought of people around the world who were falling for this trick. They had believed Nicolae wanted peace. They completely trusted the Global Community to fix their problems and take care of them. They were even buying the Global Community's religion, which taught that everyone could have their own beliefs, except those who really wanted to know the God of the Bible.

"We must not let a few bugs steal our commitment to our new world," Nicolae continued. "There will be those who will say this is a sign from the heavens. We are bad people who need to be punished.

"I ask you, what kind of god would punish people for trying to do the best they can? We have survived many disasters. It is time to put aside this silly talk and move ahead.

"We hold our own destiny in our hands. Our plans of peace and rebuilding will continue. We will unite. I have plans for good for all citizens, and I will not rest until they become a reality."

The camera pulled back, showing the locust snuggling up to Carpathia's neck. "Now does this look like any kind of judgment from an angry God? We must not allow anyone, especially those who claim to speak for God, to take away our dream of unity and peace."

A telephone number and a Web site address flashed on the screen. "If you suspect someone you know may be working against the Global Community, please call this number or contact the Web site you see on your screen.

"And if you suspect someone you know follows the teachings of Rabbi Tsion Ben-Judah, contact us immediately. Even now we are working on ways to rehabilitate those who see the Global Community as a threat."

The scene faded to black and Nicolae's voice echoed. "Do not let your hearts be troubled, my friends. Trust in me."

Vicki couldn't stop thinking about Pete. If the Peacekeepers had caught him, they would try to get information. That meant she might never see Pete alive again. She looked out over the faces of her audience.

"Do you need to take a break?" the pastor said.

Vicki nodded. The pastor handed her a bottle of water and showed her a place to sit. "What you're saying is exactly what we need to hear," the man said. "I'm not a real pastor. I just know more than the others. They all voted me the leader." He extended a hand. "I'm Greg Sowers."

"How did you figure out the truth?" Vicki said.

"I read Tsion's Web site," Greg said, "and I remember a lot from when I was a kid. My parents took me to church every time the doors were open. I won ribbons and buttons, knew all the verses. Memory stuff was easy for me. I could look at a verse once and say it right back to my Sunday school teacher."

"So how'd you get left behind if you knew all of that?" Vicki said.

"Knowing verses about God doesn't make you a believer in him," Greg said. "I fooled a lot of people. I'd live one way at school and with my friends, then clean up my act on Sundays and Wednesday nights. I even married the preacher's daughter."

"You're kidding," Vicki said.

Greg shook his head. "I used to sit with her dad and talk about the Bible till late at night. I could really talk about God, but I didn't know him."

"How did your wife find out you weren't a true Christian?"

"She never did," Greg said. "I was such a good liar. I'd come home late without an excuse and blame her for being suspicious."

"The truth never sank in?" Vicki said.

Greg put his head against the wall of the cave. "I sat through so many services. I even took notes. But it didn't mean anything until that morning."

"The morning after the disappearances?"

Greg nodded. "I told my wife I had to work overtime, but I was really out partying with some friends. I slipped into bed before sunrise and woke up late. Her nightclothes were in the bed beside me, but I didn't think anything was wrong. Then I heard the news and realized she was gone."

"That's when you prayed?" Vicki said.

Greg shook his head. "I was mad at God. Cussed him out. Then I came to my senses. I didn't have a choice. It was either ask God to forgive me or wind up following the devil's guy." Greg pointed to his forehead. "You can see what I chose."

"I'm glad you did," Vicki said.

"Now will you tell us what's next?" Greg said.

Vicki sighed. "I can, but it's not going to be easy."

✳

Judd and the others talked about Nicolae's message. "For all their talk of tolerance, it sounds like they want to wipe out any resistance to the GC," Judd said.

Pavel nodded. "Exactly. And if they can turn citizens into GC bloodhounds to sniff out believers, what hope do we have?"

"We have this hope," Judd said. "No matter how many times Nicolae quotes the Bible as if he made it up, in the end, God wins."

Lionel held up a hand and pointed to the television. "Something's going on in Maryland. Turn up the sound."

The report showed someone under a huge cover being shoved into a GC Peacekeeper cruiser. Pavel turned up the sound.

". . . has been identified as former senator

from Maryland, Chris Traickin," the news anchor said. "Traickin is suspected of subversion against the Global Community, running a religious organization that worked directly against Nicolae Carpathia and the Global Community.

"Peacekeepers equipped in special protective gear conducted the raid on Traickin's apartment and a nearby meeting place filled to capacity with followers of Rabbi Tsion Ben-Judah. It's not yet known how many others were arrested."

"I wonder how much more of that we're going to see," Judd said.

"Too much," Pavel said.

※

Someone handed Vicki a Bible and she read from Revelation 9. " 'Then locusts came from the smoke and descended on the earth, and they were given power to sting like scorpions. They were told not to hurt the grass or plants or trees but to attack all the people who did not have the seal of God on their foreheads. They were told not to kill them but to torture them for five months with agony like the pain of scorpion stings. In those days people will seek death but will not find it.' "

Vicki looked up. "We know this has been

going on for some time. People are still being stung and a lot of them have tried to kill themselves but can't.

"Everything that's been predicted in Revelation has been right on schedule. The locusts are part of the fifth Trumpet Judgment. Now comes the sixth."

Vicki paused. People scooted closer to make sure they could hear. "I don't exactly know how it's going to work, and I don't think Dr. Ben-Judah does either, but there's going to be an army of 200 million mounted troops let loose on the earth."

"You mean people on horses," a boy said, "or could these be military machines?"

"I guess they could be machines of some sort," Vicki said, "but if the locusts were real, my guess is that these are too, only bigger."

"What do the horsemen do?" someone said.

"That's the awful part. Dr. Ben-Judah has said that only one-fourth of the people left behind at the Rapture will survive until the Glorious Appearing. But this judgment is worse than anything we've seen so far. This army is going to kill a third of everybody still left on earth."

"A third?" a woman said, trembling.

Vicki nodded. "And the Bible makes it clear that most of the people who come out of this alive will continue to reject God. They'll keep on doing the evil things they've been doing."

Greg Sowers stood. "You've heard me talk about the harvest of souls that God wants to bring during this time. Well, that time is almost up. If you have loved ones or friends who are still alive, you need to get the message to them quickly."

Conrad ran into the cave out of breath. He bent over, grabbed his side, and gasped, "Somebody's coming up the trail!"

FIVE

Turmoil at the Schoolhouse

VICKI pulled Conrad aside and whispered, "Do you think it's the GC?"

"I couldn't tell," Conrad said, trying to catch his breath. "I heard them and ran up here."

Groups of believers gathered to pray. A shadow appeared at the entrance to the cave. It was Roger Cornwell from the gas station. He dropped a heavy sack as Vicki rushed to him and asked about Pete.

"The GC flew past in those vans a few minutes after Pete left," Roger said. "I don't think he could have outrun them."

"Where would they take him?" Conrad said.

Greg Sowers stepped forward. "I hope you're not thinking of trying to free your friend. You'll get in trouble. Besides, we don't know if he's been caught."

"What do we do?" Vicki said.

"Wait here," Roger said. "The GC will come back and question me. I'll let you know what I find out."

Roger left as the sun was going down. Vicki, Shelly, and Conrad huddled in a corner of the cave.

"Wonder if those people in Maryland are OK?" Conrad said.

"We did all we could," Shelly said.

Vicki shook her head. "All our stuff was with Pete. If the GC get our computer, they could find out about the Young Trib Force."

"Pete's been through this before," Conrad said. "He'll be OK."

"I should have stayed with him," Vicki said.

Shelly changed the subject. "These people were sure hungry to hear what you said."

"They're starved for information," Vicki said. "Now they know what's coming."

Two teenagers tried to start a fire, but Greg made them put it out. "No fires! The GC will see the smoke."

Someone opened the sack Roger had left and found cheese, crackers, and fruit. They all ate hungrily.

"I don't know about you," Vicki said, "but I'm going to find Pete as soon as it gets dark."

"The less time I spend in one of these caves, the better," Shelly said.

"I'm in too," Conrad said.

***

Mark followed the news about the former senator from Maryland and was sad to see how many believers had been arrested. Mark had left a phone message at Traickin's apartment, but it hadn't helped. As he scanned articles he found on the Internet, he knew something was wrong.

After Lenore put Tolan down for the night, Mark gathered all the believers together. "If the GC had found believers in Tennessee, it would probably be all over the news," Mark said.

"What do you think they'll do with the Traickin guy?" Darrion said.

Mark flipped through some news files on the computer and shook his head. "Something's not right with that story. Before the disappearances, this guy was constantly in the news. He was against President Fitzhugh about the military. They caught him with campaign money and somehow he wiggled out of it. Then the disappearances happened and Carpathia came to power."

"What did Traickin say about that?" Darrion said.

"He supported Nicolae at the start," Mark said, "but look at this." Mark turned the screen so everyone could see the story.

Traickin Urges a Return to God

While politicians and citizens alike have fallen in love with the Secretary General of the United Nations, Nicolae Carpathia, Senator Chris Traickin has fallen in love with God.

No stranger to controversy and scandal, Traickin says he believes America and the world may be following an evil man.

"We have the Pied Piper from Romania here," Traickin said in an interview from his home in Maryland. "This guy is not a friend of God-fearing Americans."

"Well, he was sure right about that," Darrion said.

"Now look at this," Mark said, clicking on another news story. "A week before that story ran, Traickin had a meeting with Carpathia. Then, after World War III breaks out, his name shows up in connection with the militia uprising."

"So the guy who fought Fitzhugh about

the military winds up being part of the militia?" Darrion said.

"Yeah, and you know what happened to the militia," Mark said.

"It got toasted by GC troops," Darrion said.

"Right," Mark said. "A few months later, Traickin shows up in another story that says he reads Tsion Ben-Judah every day and he's looking for people who want to stand up against the Global Community."

"I don't get it," Darrion said.

Charlie sat forward. "You think this guy is working for Carpathia?"

"Bingo," Mark said. "Buck Williams talked about Nicolae's mind-control tricks. What if he got to Traickin?"

"You mean he ratted on the militia and now he's working against believers?" Darrion said.

"Right," Mark said.

"How do you know you're right?" Lenore said.

"Does the way Traickin talks sound like any believers you know?" Mark said. "I think this guy was setting a trap and he succeeded."

"Then why did the GC take him off in handcuffs?" Lenore said.

"It's part of the act," Mark said.

Lenore sighed. "I don't know whether I ought to be praying for that guy or praying against him."

Charlie stood and walked toward the stairs. "Do you guys smell that?"

"What?" Mark said.

Something dripped from the ceiling. Charlie touched a drop and sniffed it. "Gasoline!"

Mark looked at Darrion and the others. "Janie and Melinda!"

Mark took the stairs three at a time and burst into Janie's room. The girl turned a gas can in her hands. She threw it but Mark ducked. Melinda lay on her bed, dazed. The room smelled like a gas station.

"What are you doing?" Mark shouted.

Janie opened a box of matches. "I'm going to end this, and there's nothing you can do to stop me!"

Judd awoke early the next morning to the phone ringing. Mr. Rudja said, "It's for you."

Judd staggered to the phone. It was Nada. "I thought Mac made it clear we shouldn't—"

"I have to see you," Nada said. "It's urgent."

"My friend is dying," Judd said. "I can't just run out on him."

"Please," Nada said. "I can't talk on the phone. There's a park a few blocks from you. Meet me there in a half hour."

※

Vicki tried to sleep but couldn't. Greg Sowers found her. "We could sure use someone like you around here if you thought you could stay."

"I have to find out what happened to Pete," Vicki said, "then we need to get back to Illinois."

"I understand," Greg said, "but I want you to know we'll make a place for you and your friends to stay for as long as you'd like."

After dark, Vicki, Conrad, and Shelly slipped out, one by one, and met near a grove of pine trees on the hillside. The sky was overcast and the wind had picked up.

"Wish we had a flashlight," Shelly said after she tripped and nearly fell.

"Stay close to me," Conrad said. "I know the way."

When they made it to the bottom, Conrad led them through a field toward the gas station. The kids saw the hazy glare of lights in the distance.

They slipped through the tall grass and hid in the shadows of the station. Conrad peeked around the corner, then quickly returned. "One of those GC vans is in front."

A few minutes later the van pulled away and the kids rushed into the station. Roger Cornwell sat behind a cash register staring out the window.

"Did they catch Pete?" Vicki said.

Roger turned and glared at them. "Where are the other believers?"

"Still at the cave," Vicki said. "What about Pete?"

Roger looked away.

"Tell us!" Shelly said.

"Pete's dead," Roger said. "The truck plunged into a ravine."

"But—"

"It caught fire," Roger said. "No one could have survived that. The GC think all those believers died too. Pete bought us some time. They'll be back in the morning to inspect the wreckage, so we have to get those people out of the cave tonight."

Vicki sat down hard. They had lost one of their best friends. How would they get back home? And when the GC discovered an empty trailer, what would happen then?

"I'll go with you," Conrad said to Roger. He put a hand on Vicki's shoulder. "You and Shelly stay here."

Vicki nodded. She felt numb. It was going to be a long night.

※

Mark couldn't believe how thin Janie and Melinda had become in such a short time. The kids had given them meals but the girls didn't eat much. "You're out of your mind!" Mark yelled. "You want this whole place to go up?"

"Yeah," Janie said, "I'm going to prove you wrong. I *can* kill myself."

"You won't," Mark said, taking a step closer.

"You want to go up with us?" Janie said, holding a match next to the box.

"OK," Mark said, backing away. "Let me get everybody out of the house first. The baby's asleep downstairs."

"OK," Janie said, pulling the match away, "but you'd better not try anything."

Mark yelled for everyone to get out. Lenore ran for Tolan. When Mark was sure everyone was outside he turned to Janie. "I know you think this is the answer to your troubles, but I've been reading reports of people jumping off tall buildings, cutting their wrists, everything you can imagine. Not one of them has died, and you won't either."

"Have any of them tried to burn themselves?" Janie said.

Mark shook his head. "No, but—"

"I don't care whether it works or not," Janie said. "I want the pain to stop!"

"That's what I'm telling you," Mark said. "The pain of the locust sting isn't going away, no matter what you do. If you try this, you'll burn yourself and the school."

"That's what you care about, isn't it?" Janie said. "Your precious hideout."

"No," Mark said. He noticed Melinda shaking uncontrollably. "At least let her out before you do this."

Janie looked at Melinda. "You want to go? Then get out of here."

"Maybe Mark's right," Melinda said, standing. "This might just make things worse for us."

As Melinda passed Janie, Mark darted behind her and lunged at the matches. Janie jerked away and Mark fell to the floor.

"Not fast enough, are you?" Janie said, holding the matches over her head. "Now you're going up with me."

As she struck the match, Charlie bolted through the door and tossed a bucket of water on Janie, dousing the matches. Janie screamed and cursed at him, then tried in vain to strike another match.

Mark wrestled Janie to the floor and dragged her down the stairs. They would need to keep a tight watch on her in the future.

※

Vicki and Shelly huddled behind a counter in the truck stop. They were glad Roger had locked the front door and turned out most of the lights.

"I can't believe Pete's really gone," Vicki said. She looked at the phone on the counter. "We have to call and tell the others."

Vicki reached for the phone. Someone moved at the front door and Vicki hit the floor. She pointed toward the door and Shelly peeked over the counter. "I don't see anything."

Vicki grabbed Shelly and pulled her down just as a GC radio squawked.

SIX

Hidden Files

VICKI'S heart beat wildly. She expected a storm of GC Peacekeepers breaking into the station. Instead, someone pecked lightly on the front window.

"What in the world?" Vicki muttered, peeking around the cash register. A big man stood near the door.

"Pete!" Vicki screamed. She rushed to the door and unlocked it. "We thought you were dead!"

Pete hugged Vicki and Shelly. "They're going to have to try a lot harder than that to kill old Pete."

"What happened?" Shelly said.

"I knew those GC would be right behind me and I remembered a ravine just up the road. No guardrail or anything. I slowed down until I saw the vans in my mirrors.

I wanted to draw them away from the gas station until you guys could get to the hills."

"It worked," Vicki said, "but how did you get out?"

"I put it in neutral and let the thing go," Pete said, showing them his scratched-up arms. "Jumped out on the passenger side and rolled into a thicket.

"The GC were all over the place, scurrying around, dodging the locusts, and trying to see the truck. Fortunately it caught fire and—"

Pete was cut off by a transmission on the tiny radio he had taken from one of the Peacekeepers. "We'll head back to the gas station and set up a lookout there," a man said.

"Where's Roger?" Pete said.

"He went to get everybody out of the cave," Vicki said.

"He can't bring them back here," Pete said. "We have to stop them."

✳

Judd tried to leave Pavel's apartment quietly, but Mr. Rudja stopped him. "Where are you going?"

"I have to meet a friend at the park," Judd said.

"Sit," Mr. Rudja said. The man poured a

cup of coffee and leaned against the kitchen counter. "My son does not have much longer to live. The doctors are amazed he has held out this long."

"I'm really sorry about—"

The man held up a hand. "I realize you took a great risk coming here, but we also have taken a great risk bringing you. One slip, one mistake could mean being found out by the Global Community."

"I understand," Judd said. "I looked in on Pavel. He's resting."

"Who is it you're meeting?"

"A girl."

The man smiled. "Ah, even in the middle of the end of the world our hearts can be stirred. . . ."

Judd chuckled nervously. "I guess, sir."

"The park is a ten-minute walk," he said, pointing out the window. "If you're not back in an hour, I'll send someone—"

"I'll be back," Judd said.

The streets were nearly deserted. Every road seemed to sparkle. Glass buildings reflected the sunlight.

The park looked like Judd's idea of the Garden of Eden. There were immense trees imported from various countries. Vines, ivy, and moss hung from branches and grew on rock walls. Ponds were stocked with exotic fish from every part of the world. Colored gravel filled a jogging path that passed a lush, green field. He spotted Nada at a bench and ran to greet her.

Nada stood and hugged Judd, then gave him a kiss on the cheek. "Thank you for coming. I didn't know what to do."

Judd sat. "What's up?"

"I was questioned by a woman from the Global Community as soon as I went inside. She wanted to know why I hadn't been stung, why my family hadn't responded to the letter the potentate sent about my brother's death, all kinds of things."

"What did you tell her?"

"I was creative," Nada said with a smile, "but it's the girl I'm rooming with that has me stumped. She's loyal to Carpathia, but she's asking questions about God."

"Might be a trap."

"Her name is Kweesa Darjonelle," Nada said. "She knew my brother. I think they dated. He told her things that made her think he wasn't completely loyal to the GC."

Judd sat up. "You mean, he may have been a believer?"

"I don't know. Before he died, Kasim told me Carpathia wasn't all he said he was. I never even thought he might have believed."

"What did this Kweesa want to know?"

"She kept probing, asking what my brother was like at home, what my parents believed about Carpathia. That made me nervous."

"It should," Judd said.

"Then she handed me this." Nada pulled out a tiny computer from her handbag. "Kasim left it at her apartment the night before the earthquake."

Judd opened the computer.

"It doesn't work," Nada said. "Kweesa said there's something wrong with the power supply."

"There may be a clue in here," Judd said. "Why hasn't Kweesa been stung?"

"She hasn't gone out of her building. There's an underground tunnel from her apartment to her office."

"The GC are smarter than we think."

"She asked me this morning if I knew anything about Tsion Ben-Judah," Nada said.

"What did you tell her?"

"I didn't know what to say. I kept thinking maybe this is someone I need to tell the truth to. She seems sincere."

"But if they link you to me, and me to Pavel and his dad . . ." Judd looked around. He couldn't expose Pavel and his father.

"I wasn't followed," Nada said. She took a

breath. "I think I'm going to tell her the truth."

"I admire your faith," Judd said, "but don't talk yet. Wait and see what else she asks."

Judd glanced at a nearby building and saw two GC Peacekeepers with binoculars. One pressed his hand to an earpiece.

"Gotta go," Judd said. "I'll look this computer over and get back with you soon."

"Wait!" Nada said, but Judd was already on the jogging path, heading back to Pavel's apartment.

Vicki tried to keep up with Pete as they ran through the night. They found Roger leading a group down the hill. When Roger saw Pete, he nearly fainted. Pete told him the news and said, "You have to get back there."

"What are you going to do?" Roger said.

"Our truck's gone. We'll have to hide until we can find some new wheels."

An older woman stepped forward. "I have a pretty big house with a barn behind it. I can take at least half of you all in."

Several others chimed in and volunteered to keep people who lived too far away to walk home.

"As soon as I locate another truck," Roger said, "I'll get in touch with you."

"Good," Pete said.

Vicki and a few others followed the woman through a valley and up another ridge. "My place is just on the other side of this mountain," the woman said.

The sun was almost up when they arrived, and Vicki was exhausted.

About twenty people crowded into the woman's kitchen as she started breakfast and assigned rooms. Conrad went to the barn with a few teenage boys. Vicki and Shelly said they were too tired to eat and made their way to a musty, downstairs room with bunk beds. Vicki sneezed and pulled the covers over her head. Finally, she fell asleep.

※

The gasoline smell was so strong that Mark and the others at the schoolhouse were forced to sleep outside. Charlie kept an eye on Janie and Melinda.

The next morning the kids got to work hosing down the upstairs room. The kids voted to put Janie and Melinda downstairs where they wouldn't be able to harm themselves or anyone else.

Darrion helped Charlie and Lenore study

the Bible. The kids prayed for Vicki, Judd, and the others and asked God to protect them from the Global Community. Charlie prayed, "Please bring Vicki back so she can see I've finally understood what you did for me."

＊

Over the next few days, Judd watched Pavel's health grow worse. The boy had trouble breathing and could hardly sit up. Judd tried to start the computer Nada had given him but couldn't. Pavel asked to look at it. His skin was pale and his fingers thin as he turned the machine over.

"Looks like the solar panel," Pavel said. "It's not getting power." He showed Judd where to hook up a regular power supply. Within a few minutes the computer was working.

As Judd inspected different files, he noticed the daily entries of Nada's brother. "This is almost like a diary," Judd said. He read a few entries to Pavel.

" 'I've been assigned duty at the potentate's headquarters tomorrow,' " the boy wrote in an early entry. " 'I finally get to see things up close.*' "

Judd was puzzled. "I wonder what that

asterisk means. There's a bunch of them throughout the entries."

"Let me see," Pavel said. He raised his head and clicked through the file. "There are notes embedded in the text. Something he doesn't want anyone to see." He fiddled with the tiny keyboard and a screen popped up. "It's asking for a password. Four letters."

"What could be in those secret files?" Judd said.

Pavel shook his head and typed several words, then letters and numbers. He tried combinations using letters from the words *Global Community*, but each time the computer denied access.

"Sometimes people will use their own initials or birthdays or names of people they're close to," Pavel said. "Makes it easy to remember. What's this guy's name?"

"Kasim," Judd said. "I don't know his middle name."

Pavel typed more words but came up with nothing.

"Wait," Judd said, "his sister is Nada. Try that."

Pavel typed in her name and the computer whirred. "Bingo!"

The document revealed nearly one hundred pages of single-spaced notes Kasim had written. Pavel scrolled down and Judd read over his shoulder.

"Nada came to the training camp today and embarrassed me," Kasim wrote. "She's just as committed to her beliefs as I am to Nicolae Carpathia. I hope she'll see that she's wrong about him."

"Can you find anything else about Nada in there?" Judd said.

Pavel did a word search and came up with several more sections with Nada's name. "Here, read it to me."

Judd took the computer. " 'Talked with Nada today about the facilities here. There is so much luxury and wealth. My room is like a palace compared to back home. Why can't my family see the truth?' "

Judd skipped to the last few pages of notes. " 'I talked with Nada tonight about seeing Leon Fortunato in the hallway of the building. It's exciting anytime I see someone famous, but I can't tell Nada what's really going on in my heart.' "

Judd scrolled up and found passages that talked about Kasim's feelings for Kweesa. Kasim mentioned another friend named Dan. " 'Dan seems to know what's going to happen before it does. He thinks there's a big earthquake coming sometime soon. I've asked how he knows all this and he's been pretty cagey.' "

The next entry talked about Dan wanting to meet with Kasim after they finished work the next day.

"What happened with that?" Pavel said.

Judd scrolled down and found the answer. " 'It was like talking to my family,' " Kasim wrote. " 'Dan believes everything they do. I tried talking some sense into him, but he wouldn't budge. He gave me a Bible but I refused. I don't know what to do. He's working for the potentate but is totally against him. I am betraying what I believe by not exposing him, but I haven't exposed my family either. What should I do?' "

Pavel put his head back. "I'd like to hear more, but I'm so tired."

"It's OK," Judd said. "Rest. I'll tell you how it ends when you wake up."

※

Vicki awoke sneezing and red eyed. She wandered upstairs around midday and found an old computer. She tried to check e-mail but couldn't.

The woman who owned the house came into the kitchen. "I don't know anything about that thing. It's my son's. He ran off a few days before the locusts came and I haven't heard from him since."

"Is he a believer?" Vicki said.

The woman wiped sweat from her face with a paper towel. "I tried to talk with him time and again. As far as I know, he's not one of us."

Vicki kept working with the computer as she listened to the woman's story. She had gone to church since she was a girl and had taken her children as well. "I always heard that going to church doesn't make you a Christian any more than walking into a garage makes you a car. I guess they were right."

Pete came into the room. "That computer's no good. I tried to get a message to the co-op but I couldn't get through. It's something with the phone lines."

"Then there's no way to get in touch with Carl or Mark," Vicki said, "or those people in Maryland."

Pete shook his head. "Local radio reported they arrested a bunch of people, including that former senator."

Vicki plopped into a chair. "The GC is getting tighter, and we're stuck."

"Yeah, we're stuck," Pete said, "but on the positive side, you've got a lot of people to teach. That pastor came by about an hour ago and asked if you'd talk to people tonight."

"If we meet, we might get caught," Vicki said.

Pete smiled. "When has that ever stopped us?"

SEVEN

Kasim's Confusion

JUDD stayed with Pavel while doctors monitored the boy's condition from remote computers. It was clear that Pavel was getting worse. While Judd waited, he read page after page of Kasim's diary. Kasim mentioned Kweesa often and wrote about missing his family in Israel as well. *Nada's parents would love to see the files*, Judd thought.

The most interesting sections detailed the turmoil Kasim experienced when he wrote about Dan. "The more I see of the Global Community and the way they treat people," Kasim wrote, "the more confused I get. They talk about tolerance, then threaten people if they visit the Ben-Judah Web site.

"I saw pictures of the two aides Peter had

executed. This guy is supposed to be the head of the one world religion. If that's the kind of religion the GC wants us to follow, I can't do it.

"Every day I think about what my family believes. If they're right, I'm working for the devil. But how could that be? Nicolae Carpathia is doing so many good things."

Kasim went back and forth with his arguments. On one page he listed the positives of both belief systems.

Global Community	My Parents' Beliefs
Nicolae Carpathia is god.	God is supreme.
Every religion has a bit of truth.	There is only one way to God.
Religion is a set of rules to follow.	You can know God personally.
Plagues are bad.	Plagues are to get our attention.
Morality is up to each person.	Truth is based on what God says.

"I want to believe what the Global Community stands for," Kasim wrote, "but something tells me my parents are right."

Judd found the entry for the night before the earthquake and read it over and over. He checked Pavel's condition and phoned Nada. "I need to see you right away."

Vicki met with members of the Johnson City underground church in the musty basement. Shelly and Conrad helped her move a mountain of canning jars and dusty boxes to make room.

About twenty people crammed into the tight space. Some sat on the floor. Others brought chairs. These people were hungry for any kind of teaching.

Vicki went over the same information she had taught Carl Meninger when he was at the schoolhouse. She referred to the notes Lenore had typed for her, but as she went over the Scriptures, she found herself relying less on notes. Things Tsion Ben-Judah had said or written came back to her, and the people were amazed such a young woman could teach so well.

Pete slipped in after the meeting and reported the latest from Roger. "As far as we can tell, the GC are gone."

"Why would they leave?" Vicki said.

"They came to the station and made a big show about pulling out," Pete said. "I guess they looked at the truck and were satisfied."

"They didn't find any bodies," Conrad said.

"I'll bet they're hiding somewhere waiting for the believers to come back for their cars."

"We'll stay here another day to make sure," Pete said. "I've got a line on another truck we can use. Our supplies from Florida are still in the parking lot of the gas station."

Vicki tried to sleep, but the dust and mildew were too much for her. After dark, she found Shelly and they walked to the backyard. They found two rickety chairs and sat near an outdoor fireplace. Vicki breathed in the cool, mountain air. An owl hooted in the distance.

"Until I met Judd," Vicki said, "I'd never lived in anything bigger than a trailer." She looked at the tree-lined mountainside and sighed. "All this space is incredible."

Shelly suggested they get some covers and try sleeping outside. Suddenly, someone cried in the distance.

"What was that?" Shelly said.

"I don't know," Vicki said, "but it didn't sound like an animal. It sounded human."

Crickets chirped and frogs croaked from a nearby pond. Vicki finally turned to go inside and heard the cry again.

Shelly pointed. "It's coming from up there."

Vicki headed up the hill. Shelly protested but finally tagged along. The two quietly made their way in the moonlight. They cautiously walked around a small pond and followed a narrow creek bed. The trees were thick and several times Vicki had to retrace her steps and go around them.

Finally, they reached a clearing and climbed through a barbed-wire fence. In the distance, a small cabin was built into the side of the hill.

"I don't like this," Shelly said. "Let's go back."

A light flickered inside. "There's somebody in there," Vicki said. "Maybe they're hurt."

"And there might be a bear or something waiting to jump out at us!"

Vicki shook her head and climbed the side of a smooth rock to the top of the ridge. The cabin was made of small logs. The holes had been filled in with mud, but the glow of a lantern shone through.

Someone inside let out a piercing scream that echoed through the valley. "Please," Shelly whispered, "let's get out of here."

"I have to see who's in there," Vicki said.

The door to the cabin burst open and someone stood in the shadows with a gun. "Who's out there?" the man shouted.

"It's OK," Vicki shouted back. "We're friends of the woman in the house at the bottom of the hill."

"You better come inside, or those stingin' bugs'll bite you."

Vicki took Shelly's hand and the two

walked into the cabin. The man was thin with a scraggly beard. He wore a dirty baseball cap pulled low. The man's eyes were red and there were beer bottles strewn about the cabin. He motioned for them to sit by the fire that burned in a pit in the middle of the room.

"You were stung, weren't you?" Vicki said.

The man pulled a blanket over his shoulders. He leaned against the wall and propped his head against a log. "What are you doing at my mother's house?"

※

Judd slipped into the back pew of the Enigma Babylon One World Cathedral, not far from Pavel's apartment. The church was a monument to every religion except Judaism and Christianity. There were statues of gods and goddesses, pictures of people on their knees before pieces of wood and stone, and framed speeches of Nicolae Carpathia. Since the attack of locusts, all services had been canceled, but the building was open to anyone. Huge, stone archways stood a hundred feet above Judd's head. Inscriptions were written on pillars throughout the sanctuary. The first said, "One world, one faith." Another simply said, "Tolerance." Still another read, "Strive for unity."

Each seat had its own interactive screen and headphones. He slipped the headphones on and watched a recording of a recent service. As the "Veneration Leader" sang and read "holy texts," Judd followed the words as they flashed on the screen. He scrolled through the service and found a message by Pontifex Maximus Peter Mathews. Several times during the message people were asked to give an opinion on a religious question by touching the screen.

"How can a person find the true way to spirituality and inner peace?" Pontifex Mathews said. "*(a)* by following a list of rules and regulations, *(b)* by following someone who says there is only one way to God, or *(c)* by following your own beliefs and letting your heart be your guide."

The audience had unanimously chosen "c." As he scrolled through the rest of the message, Nada slipped in beside him. "How is Pavel?" she whispered.

Judd frowned. "He's getting worse."

"Why did you want to meet here?" Nada said.

"I think we were being watched at the park." Judd handed Nada a printout of some of the pages from Kasim's hidden journal. "There may be a chance Kasim became a believer before the earthquake."

Nada was obviously moved by the words of her brother. She scanned the pages.

Judd finally took them from her and said, "There's only one person who could know whether your brother became a believer before he died. It's this guy, Dan."

"Maybe Kweesa knows him," Nada said.

"For all we know, he could have died in the earthquake, but we have to find out. If you can take home proof that your brother became a believer, your dad won't be so mad at you."

"I'll go right now," Nada said.

Nada rushed out and Judd continued scrolling through the sermon archives. The last recording was made the day of the locust attack. Judd clicked it and up popped the video of Pontifex Maximus Peter Mathews at the podium. He was in his full outfit, complete with the huge hat and long robes. Judd couldn't resist. He turned the sound up and put on the headphones.

"Some in our world have the mistaken notion that we are wrong," Peter said. "They believe in an angry, mean-spirited god who would punish people. I ask you, is this the kind of god you want?"

Peter waited as people locked in their responses. A number flashed on the screen and the man smiled. "One hundred percent of you agree that god is not like that."

Judd noticed a humming in the background. As it grew louder, he realized what was coming.

Peter threw his arms open wide. "God is here right now with you and me." He placed his hands over his heart. "God is in us! We are god!"

Someone screamed in the back of the church. Peter tried to calm the people, but off camera the droning of wings and shrill voices of locusts overtook the congregation.

Peter stepped from behind the podium and the camera panned the frantic crowd. The locusts attacked people at will, stinging them and sending them to the floor.

"Don't panic!" Peter screamed. The camera focused on him just as several locusts flew his way. He screamed and threw his hat at the beasts, cursing. He pulled his thick robes over his head and fell.

A locust found the exposed flesh of Peter's leg. Judd hadn't seen such a vivid picture of a person being stung before. The camera zoomed in as the beast threw its head back and bared its fangs. It sent the demonic venom deep into the bloodstream of the thrashing Pontifex Maximus. The camera swiveled wildly and the transmission went dead.

Vicki introduced herself and the man said his name was Omer. He had been bitten when the locusts had first come. He was in great pain, but it seemed to be getting a little better.

"My mother was on me every day about religion," he said. "I knew I had to get away or I'd go crazy. I went to stay with a friend and started drinking. His dad threw me out, so I bought some booze and came up here."

As Vicki's eyes grew accustomed to the dim light, she saw piles of bottles stacked around the room. "Does drinking make it less painful?"

Omer shook his head. "I can't even get drunk. I try but it doesn't have the same effect."

"What do you think of your mom's religion now?" Shelly said.

Omer frowned. "I just want to be left alone. Is that so much to ask?"

"Your mom is worried," Vicki said. "You should let her know where you are."

"She'd be up here with a bunch of you people trying to get me to change my mind."

Vicki sighed. She wanted to talk with Omer about God, but he wasn't ready. "Your mom says that's your computer in the kitchen. Are you any good with it?"

"It's about all I am good at," Omer said.

"I'm trying to get a message to some friends but I can't hook up," Vicki said. "Can you help?"

Omer scratched his beard. "If you don't tell anybody about me, I'll meet you at the back door tomorrow night."

***

Judd grew concerned when Nada didn't return. Had she asked Kweesa too many questions? Maybe the GC was onto her.

He found a phone and called the apartment. A woman answered on the third ring.

"Kweesa?" Judd said.

"You must be Judd," the woman said. "Nada told me you might call. Something terrible has happened."

"What's wrong?"

"Nada came a few minutes ago and asked a lot of questions about Kasim's friend Dan. I told her everything I knew, but I don't think I should have."

"Why?"

"Dan was arrested a few weeks ago," Kweesa said. "He's in a GC prison."

"Arrested for what?" Judd said.

"Subversion," Kweesa said. "I don't know what he did, but Nada is in real danger."

"Where is she?" Judd yelled.

"She's gone to the prison to see him!"

EIGHT

Dan's Riddle

JUDD couldn't believe Nada had gone to a GC prison, but since Kweesa wasn't a believer, he tried to act calm. "Why are you upset with Nada?"

"First of all, she took my car keys and ran out," Kweesa said. "She's going to get stung. And second, if she does make it to the prison, this Dan guy is off-limits. He must have done something really bad and the guards might think she's mixed up with him."

"She's grieving her brother," Judd said. "She wants information. Won't they understand?"

Kweesa paused. "I don't think so."

"I'll try to stop her," Judd said. He asked directions to the prison and ran into the street to hail a cab, but there were none. When he reached Pavel's apartment, he found the elevators were out of service. Judd raced to the stairs.

Mr. Rudja put up a hand when Judd rushed into the room. "Quiet. The doctors are doing more tests on Pavel."

Judd caught his breath and quickly explained the situation. "Will the GC let her in to talk with him?"

Pavel's father groaned and shut his eyes. "Daniel Nieters is a restricted case. Only a few people know the charges against him."

"What did he do?" Judd said.

"He's a believer. He spoke with someone in Leon Fortunato's office about God and the person turned him in."

"Wouldn't the GC want to make an example of him in public?"

"Fortunately, Leon was embarrassed that a Judah-ite was working for them. I think he kept it quiet from the potentate for a while. They put Dan away and made the information classified."

"So there's no way they're going to let her talk to him," Judd said.

Mr. Rudja picked up the phone. "Dan is in isolation so he can't talk with anyone, but security will detain and question anyone who asks for him."

While Mr. Rudja talked on the phone, Judd checked on Pavel. Lionel and Sam sat quietly in the room as a doctor examined him from a remote location.

"Have you ever seen anything like that?" Lionel whispered as the probe scanned Pavel's body. "House calls without leaving the hospital."

Lionel and Sam joined Judd in the next room. Judd explained what he had discovered on Kasim's computer and where Nada had gone.

Lionel rolled his eyes. "More trouble. I thought Mac told her to play it safe."

"I can understand why she's excited," Sam said. "If I thought a relative of mine might have become a believer before he died, I'd want to know."

"Yeah," Lionel said, "but find out in heaven. Don't risk your life and everybody else's."

Pavel gave a cry and his father hurried into the room. As he passed, he handed Judd a set of car keys and said, "Wait here a moment."

"I'm going with you," Lionel said.

"Me too," Sam said.

Judd convinced Sam to stay and help. Mr. Rudja walked slowly out of the bedroom. He rubbed his face with both hands and sat heavily on the couch. "Take the car and go to the prison. I've explained to the warden how emotional the girl is and he's agreed to let her talk with Dan. They'll keep her in the waiting room until you get there."

"How'd you manage that?" Judd said.

"It was more an order than a request," Mr. Rudja said. "Tell her all conversations are recorded. Be extremely careful about what you say."

Judd nodded. "Is something else wrong?"

"It's Pavel. The report is not good. He might not be with us much longer."

Judd's heart sank. He wanted to know more, but Mr. Rudja pushed him toward the door. "Hurry to the prison and bring Nada back safely. I'll tell you about Pavel when you return."

Lionel agreed to ride with Judd and return Mr. Rudja's car. Judd was in a daze as they drove to the prison.

"I have to tell you," Lionel said, "I don't like the way this is working."

"I didn't ask Nada to come," Judd said.

"Didn't say you did. But you're encouraging her. She's talking about marriage."

"So?"

"It's crazy! You're not ready for that."

"Let's talk later," Judd said. "I have to get Nada out of there and try to get back to Pavel."

Lionel stared out the window.

"What?" Judd said.

"When you want to shut people down you always say you want to talk later."

A sign pointed the way to the prison. Judd expected an imposing building on the outskirts of town with razor wire and guards every ten feet. Instead, the building was stately, with a sprawling lawn surrounded by a stone wall. It wasn't until he pulled up to the entrance that he noticed the electronic sensors inside the compound.

Judd got out. "You'll be OK?"

"Yeah," Lionel said as he drove away.

Judd walked to the front gate and said his name into a speaker. A man told him to come to the parking garage and follow signs for building "B."

Judd walked through a series of secured doors. A guard met him and looked surprised that Judd hadn't been stung. The deputy warden shook hands with Judd and showed him to a waiting room where Nada sat alone. When she saw Judd, she stood and hugged him. The deputy warden gave them a few instructions. "We'll call you when the prisoner is ready."

"I'm sorry I didn't come back for you," Nada said after the man left. "When I found out where Dan was, I—"

"It's all right," Judd said. "I understand."

Judd put his face close to Nada's ear and whispered, "Don't say anything you wouldn't want Nicolae Carpathia himself to hear. Mr. Rudja says we'll be monitored in every room. We have to be careful with Dan or we could all wind up in this place."

Nada stepped back, a look of horror on her face. "I've done it again, haven't I?"

Judd leaned close. "Play up your emotions. We've convinced them you're here to find out about your brother and that you're ticked at Dan for trying to lead him astray."

Nada immediately burst into tears. She put her head on Judd's chest and said, "Why did he have to die?"

Judd played along. "It's been a long time since the earthquake. You need to move on."

"Oh yeah? Did you have a family member die in the quake?"

"No."

"Then don't tell me to move on! I miss him. I want to know what happened. They never found his body!"

Nada collapsed into a chair and Judd sat beside her. "Good stuff," he whispered. "Keep it up."

"If they're listening to us, how are we going to talk to Dan?" Nada whispered.

"We just let him talk," Judd said.

The deputy warden returned and escorted

them into a small room with a table and three chairs. There were two huge mirrors on each side of the room.

Moments later the door opened and a man in shackles shuffled in. He looked to be in his twenties and wore handcuffs around his wrists. His face was swollen and bruised. Though the man's face was discolored, Judd could still see the mark of the believer plainly on his forehead.

The man sat and leaned back in his chair. When he saw Judd and Nada's marks, he smiled. The guard left and closed the door.

"Who are you?" the man barked.

Judd leaned forward. "Are you Dan Nieters?"

"You know who I am—now what do you want?" Dan said.

Judd was glad Dan was speaking gruffly. He surely had no idea who they were and what they wanted, but if he kept this act up, they might make it out OK.

Nada leaned forward and shouted, "You knew my brother! Kasim!"

Dan caught his breath and shifted in his chair. "Yeah, I knew him. We worked security. He was in the Administration Building when it came down. I'm sorry for your loss."

Nada chose her words carefully. "My

brother was devoted to the Global Community. You tried to take him away with your foolish ideas, didn't you?!"

Dan squirmed in his seat. He looked like he was searching for the right words.

"My family didn't get to say good-bye," Nada said. "Were you with him before he died?"

Dan stared at them. Finally, he said, "Jesus is Lord."

"Don't give us that!" Judd said.

"'God so loved the world that he gave his only Son. . . .'"

Someone moved in the next room. Dan glanced at a mirror. The door to the room burst open and a guard grabbed Dan and pulled him to his feet.

"I tell you the same thing the angel said to the women who came to the tomb!" Dan shouted. "Matthew 7:7!"

The guard pulled Dan from the room and slammed the door. Nada put her head on the table. A few moments later the door opened and the deputy warden joined them. He held up his hands in disgust. "I'm sorry you had to hear that. You can see what we have to deal with."

Nada sobbed. "Why did he speak that way? Why couldn't he tell me something?"

"This man is a religious zealot," the deputy

warden said. "I knew he wouldn't cooperate, but I understand you had to try."

When they were in the car, Nada said, "What do you think Dan meant?"

Judd put a finger to his lips. He drove through the gate and a few minutes later pulled to the curb and stopped. Judd searched under the seats and throughout the car. "I want to make sure they didn't plant some kind of listening device. He was definitely trying to send us a message, but he knew we'd be in big trouble if we just talked."

"I don't get it," Nada said. "Was he saying Kasim became a believer?"

"I'm not sure," Judd said.

Judd took Nada to Pavel's apartment and told the others what had happened. Mr. Rudja had called the prison shortly after Judd and Nada left. "You did well. They don't suspect anything."

Judd repeated exactly what Dan had said.

Lionel grabbed a Bible and opened to the book of Matthew. "Let's assume he was trying to tell you something and the 'Jesus is Lord' was him getting the GC's attention off of you.

"The second part is from John 3:16," Lionel continued. "It's probably the most famous verse in the Bible."

"Do you think that means Kasim became a believer?" Nada said.

"It's a good guess," Judd said, "but maybe there's more."

"Yeah," Lionel said as he flipped pages, "the next part is about what the angel said to the women at the tomb."

Lionel searched passages in all four Gospels and concluded that Dan had to be talking about Luke 24. The kids gathered around and read the passage.

"But very early on Sunday morning the women came to the tomb, taking the spices they had prepared. They found that the stone covering the entrance had been rolled aside. So they went in, but they couldn't find the body of the Lord Jesus. They were puzzled, trying to think what could have happened to it. Suddenly, two men appeared to them, clothed in dazzling robes. The women were terrified and bowed low before them. Then the men asked, 'Why are you looking in a tomb for someone who is alive? He isn't here! He has risen from the dead!' "

Nada smiled. "That's it! Dan was telling us that though Kasim died in the earthquake, he's alive spiritually. He must have believed!"

"Maybe," Judd said, "but Dan could have come right out and said that and not endangered us."

"Maybe the answer is in the last verse Dan gave you," Lionel said. He opened the Bible to Matthew 7:7.

" 'Keep on asking, and you will be given what you ask for. Keep on looking, and you will find. Keep on knocking, and the door will be opened.' "

"I know he's telling us that Kasim became a believer!" Nada said.

An alarm rang in Pavel's room. Judd ran to the boy's side and found Mr. Rudja on his knees by the bed. Doctors in the monitor barked orders.

Pavel's face was ashen. His pulse was weak and erratic. Suddenly, the line went flat and the machine sounded a piercing beep.

"Do something!" Judd yelled.

NINE

The Escape

WHILE Shelly kept watch for anyone moving around the house, Vicki met Omer at the back door. He looked around the kitchen nervously. "You sure my mom didn't put you up to this?"

Vicki shook her head and whispered, "I didn't tell her anything. Everybody's asleep except for our friend Pete. He's at the gas station."

Omer sat in front of the screen and entered a few codes.

"Where did you learn to type that fast?" Vicki said.

"Just because I'm from Tennessee doesn't mean I'm stupid," Omer said.

"I didn't mean it that way," Vicki said.

Omer winced in pain from the locust bite and pointed to the screen. "I put a block in here on the satellite phone."

"You have a satphone?" Vicki said.

"One of the toys I was into back when the disappearances happened," Omer said. He changed some codes and tried to dial. "Who are you trying to reach?" Omer said.

"Some friends in Illinois," Vicki said. "We haven't had contact with them since—"

The back door opened and Pete walked in, out of breath. Vicki introduced Omer, who stood to leave.

"Stay where you are," Pete said to Omer. He looked at Vicki and Shelly. "You'll be glad to know our new rig is lined up. We can head out tomorrow morning."

Omer continued working, determined to fix the problem. He grabbed a screwdriver and took the back off the computer. As he tinkered with the inside, Vicki saw someone out of the corner of her eye.

"O?"

Omer turned. "Mom."

The woman, in her bathrobe, hugged her son and wept. "I didn't know if I'd ever see you again."

Omer looked at the floor.

"It's OK," his mother said. "What's important is that you're back."

"I'm not staying."

The woman looked stunned. She glanced

at Vicki and Shelly. "I must look a mess. Let me get you all something to eat."

"I'm not hungry," Omer said. "I'm just going to get this computer going for these girls; then I'm leaving."

Vicki and Shelly turned to leave.

"Don't go," Omer said. "I'm going to hook you up with your friends."

※

Judd and the others stayed outside Pavel's room as the doctors gave instructions to Mr. Rudja. Judd wanted to run for a doctor or get some medicine. All he could do was wait.

A few minutes later, Pavel's father walked slowly out of the room.

"Is he . . . ?" Judd said, but he couldn't finish the sentence.

"The doctors have him stabilized," Mr. Rudja said, "but he's unconscious."

Nada put a hand to her mouth. "Oh no!"

"He may come out of it," Mr. Rudja said, "or he could slip into a coma. They're sending a helicopter to take him to the hospital."

Judd felt guilty for not spending more time with Pavel. He had been so concerned about Nada and finding out about her brother that he hadn't been there for Pavel.

Mr. Rudja put a hand on Judd's shoulder.

"Would you mind staying with him while I prepare for the transport?"

"Sure," Judd said.

The man paused. "You coming here has been a great gift to Pavel."

"I could have done more," Judd said.

Mr. Rudja shook his head. "You may still have a chance."

❋

Late at night Mark watched for news coming from the Global Community about Johnson City, Tennessee. *No news is good news*, he thought. Several times Mark had written Vicki but there was no answer. He tried contacting Pete in the truck but got a recorded message.

Charlie joined Mark and the two scanned the latest news stories. Mark was amazed at how much Charlie had changed since understanding the message and becoming a true believer. He seemed more confident.

A bulletin from the East Coast GC headquarters in Baltimore popped up on the screen. A picture of Chris Traickin accompanied the flash. Underneath the photo was the word *Escaped*.

"Former Senator Chris Traickin, arrested for subversive activities with a group of religious rebels near Baltimore, attacked two Global Community Peacekeepers and escaped early today in a specially equipped GC van. The suspect is considered armed and dangerous.

"Officials say Traickin overpowered two Peacekeepers who were transporting him to a different holding facility.

"Anyone who sees Traickin is urged to avoid confrontation and phone Global Community officials immediately," the report said.

"Wow," Charlie said, "that's great!"

Mark frowned. "It's not right."

"What do you mean?" Charlie said. "He got away from the GC! That's good, isn't it?"

Mark turned to Charlie. "Think about it. He got loose this morning and they're reporting it now?"

"Maybe they just found out."

"If he'd really overpowered two Peacekeepers *and* stolen a van, it would have been all over the news as soon as it happened. Doesn't make sense."

"You think they let him loose? Why would they do that?"

Mark shook his head.

"Isn't there a chance that you're wrong?" Charlie said. "Maybe this guy is a true believer—"

"The whole Traickin thing stinks," Mark said. He turned back to the keyboard and quickly typed an e-mail. "Maybe Carl can find out what's going on."

Charlie sat back. He scrunched his eyebrows.

"What?" Mark said.

"I feel like we need to pray for Vicki."

※

While Omer worked on the computer, Vicki asked his mother to step into the next room. "I know this isn't really any of my business, but I think Omer just needs to be left alone for a while."

The woman turned. "How could you possibly know what's best for my boy?"

"He talked to us about what happened to him after the Rapture," Vicki said. "I think he's coming around to the truth."

"If he would have realized the truth sooner, he wouldn't have been stung by those locusts," the woman whispered.

"I know," Vicki said, "but if you keep after him, you're going to drive him away. I think deep down he knows what you're saying is true, but he has to accept it for himself. I'm afraid he's going to hide again."

"Where?" the woman said.

"I promised I wouldn't say," Vicki said.

The woman looked away. "I've heard him out there in the middle of the night. He must live like an animal." She turned to Vicki. "Do you know the story of that guy in the Old Testament who went crazy and lived out in the wild?"

Vicki shrugged. "Don't think I've read that one yet."

"He had a really long name. He wouldn't give God the credit he deserved, so God made him eat grass like a cow. He went crazy and I think that's what's happening now. God's trying to get my son's attention one more time. I just don't want him to miss it."

Vicki nodded. "He knows the truth. It's up to him."

The woman nodded and went back to the kitchen. Omer didn't look up from his work. His mother put a plate near the keyboard and leaned close. "You're welcome to stay here anytime you like. I'm praying for you, and I still love you."

With that, she kissed her son on the forehead and went back to her room. Omer didn't turn around until she had closed the door. He glanced at Vicki. "She does make a pretty mean ham sandwich. Just wish I felt hungry enough to enjoy it."

Vicki smiled. "Any progress?"

Omer took a bite of the sandwich. "Get some sleep. If I figure it out, I'll wake you."

Vicki thanked him and headed down the hall.

"And, Vicki," Omer said, "thanks."

***

Judd sat by Pavel's bed as Sam and Lionel helped get things ready for the helicopter flight. Judd picked up Pavel's lifeless hand and squeezed it. He hung his head and prayed silently for the boy.

God, I don't know why you would allow something like this to happen. I guess there are some things I'll never understand until I get to heaven. You must have some kind of purpose for putting Pavel through this. I pray you'd help the doctors figure out what to do. Help his dad . . .

Judd finished his prayer and turned to the computer. In Pavel's e-mail were scores of messages from people around the world who had written about the gospel. As Judd read further, it became clear. Pavel had led many people to the truth about God. Pavel had hardly any strength, but what he had he used for God.

Someone moved behind Judd. It was Pavel.

"Thought you could read my mail while I was out of it, huh?" Pavel said weakly.

"Let me get your father," Judd said. "The helicopter will be here soon."

"Wait," Pavel said. "I want to talk."

Pavel closed his eyes and motioned Judd closer. He spoke just above a whisper. "I dreamed last night that I saw my mother in heaven." The boy smiled. "We ran together and laughed." Pavel's eyes filled with tears. "Remember when I said God was going to heal me?"

Judd nodded.

"It's true. He's going to give me the ultimate healing. He's going to take me home."

"You're going to be OK," Judd said. "Just rest."

Pavel leaned forward. "The message from Dan. The sayings from the Bible."

"You heard us talking about that?"

"Sure, I heard everything. I just couldn't respond."

"What do you think it means?" Judd said.

"I think Dan was trying to tell you something more. Find out where Dan lives. Go there."

"That would almost be suicide, wouldn't it?"

"Perhaps," Pavel said, "but there is a

reason Dan spoke in a riddle. Ask. Look. Knock."

Judd nodded. He noticed Mr. Rudja in the next room and called for him.

"There's one more thing," Pavel said. "God is going to heal me soon."

"Yeah," Judd said.

Pavel smiled as his father hugged him and whispered something to the boy. Judd slipped out of the room and left them alone. The helicopter came a few minutes later and carried him away.

*

Vicki and the others were ready to leave the next morning, but Omer was still working on the computer. His mother sipped coffee at the kitchen table.

"I thought I had it a few minutes ago," Omer said.

Vicki put a hand on his shoulder. "We're headed home. We'll get in touch with our friends on the way."

Omer looked up and winced in pain. "Once I get it in my head to fix something, I can't hardly stop."

Vicki typed a message to Mark and the others back at the schoolhouse. "If you do get through, send this to them."

Omer promised and walked them outside. He showed Pete a shortcut to the gas station through a wooded area. Omer turned to Vicki. "I've been thinking about all the stuff you told me about God."

"You mean the stuff I tried to tell you," Vicki said, smiling.

"Yeah. Well, maybe when I feel better I'll give it another shot."

"I hope you will," Vicki said, "but don't wait."

Omer nodded. "I'll keep trying to hook up with your friends."

Vicki looked back as they walked into the woods. Omer stood on the front porch, waving.

TEN

Looking for Believers

AT THE schoolhouse, Mark continued his work on the kids' Web site, www.the-underground-online.com. More and more young people wrote each day with questions and messages of encouragement. Mark took Tsion Ben-Judah's latest e-mails and helped kids understand them. Even adults who had written said they had been helped by the site.

Vicki hadn't checked in, but Mark hoped she was OK. He was excited to find a message from Tom and Luke Gowin in South Carolina. They thanked Vicki and the others for their teaching.

We all feel like we're better able to stay out of the GC's way and spread the message, Tom wrote.

Another message caught his eye. Mr. Stein

wrote the kids from Africa. *God is doing wonderful things here. I can't wait to see you all in person so I can explain. As soon as I can travel to Israel or back home, I'll let you know.*

While he was reading, an urgent message came from Carl Meninger in Florida. Mark hooked up the videoconferencing feature and seconds later saw Carl. He was in his room at the GC compound in Florida. Carl looked tired.

"Everything OK?" Mark said.

"I worked all night and you're not going to believe what I found out," Carl said.

Carl explained that two GC Peacekeepers were stung by locusts in Tennessee. "The guys could hardly talk, but they said a red-haired girl and a big truck driver were responsible."

"Vicki and Pete!" Mark said.

"All the believers got away," Carl said.

"Are the Peacekeepers still looking for them?"

"I talked with one guy involved in Tennessee this morning. He said they're waiting for some kind of secret operation, but he doesn't know what it is. He told me they're going to get these people just like they did in Baltimore."

"I read about that," Mark said.

"Here's the weird part. You know that former senator you asked me about?"

"Traickin?" Mark said.

"Right. Well, it turns out the guy's a fake. Somehow he got hooked up with a group of believers and he got them arrested."

"How could he fake his mark and escape the locusts?"

"You got me," Carl said. "And one more thing—"

"Let me guess," Mark interrupted. "The story about him escaping is fake too."

"Right. And if there's one imposter working for the GC, there have to be others."

"Which means we have to warn people about the possibility of moles like Traickin," Mark said.

"Put it on your Web site and do everything you can to get the word out," Carl said. "As time goes on and the effect of the locust stings wear off, the GC will arrest anyone who sides with Dr. Ben-Judah."

"Which means you being inside the GC is even more important," Mark said, "and even more dangerous. Any other believers down there?"

"Haven't seen any," Carl said. "One day they'll ask me to bow down to Carpathia's picture or some statue and I'll have to get out. But for now, think of me as your eyes and ears inside the belly of the beast."

Vicki followed Pete and Shelly as they hiked through the woods. Conrad was last in line. He told Vicki what he had learned about the Tennessee believers.

"I'd say about nine out of ten people I talked with had gone to church before the disappearances," Conrad said. "Some of them were even regular attenders."

"Why didn't they believe?" Vicki said.

Conrad shrugged. "I guess you have to do more than just show up. God offers a gift, but you still have to receive it."

Conrad asked Vicki about Omer. Vicki explained how they had met and what had kept him from believing. "Some people are stubborn. Others have pet sins they don't want to give up. But I think a lot of people have never seen anyone have a real relationship with God."

Pete stopped at the top of a knoll and asked the kids to be quiet. He pointed to a red truck hitched to a trailer. "That has all our supplies from Florida. I'm going to see if Roger will let us leave it here to feed the believers in Johnson City."

"You think the GC is still around?" Conrad said.

Pete nodded. "One of the kids rode to the

bowling alley and said there's at least one van still there."

"I wish we could get our motorcycle back," Vicki said.

"If that's the biggest sacrifice we make, I'll be happy," Pete said.

Shelly said, "Why do you think they held back? They could have sent out search parties and questioned people."

"Roger said they stopped by his place a couple of times," Pete said. "But you're right; it doesn't make sense."

Pete led them to a back entrance of the gas station. As usual, only a handful of people were in the diner. Pete found Roger and discussed the food shipment. Roger said they would organize a group to come during the night and transfer the food to the cave and a few nearby houses.

"You're fueled up and ready to go," Roger said.

Vicki hugged the man and thanked him. "I hope we get back here again."

"Me too," Roger said. "You guys saved us. And everyone's said good things about your teaching. We can't thank you enough."

Roger handed Vicki a paper bag. "You'll find some goodies for your trip in the sack. God bless you."

Pete told the kids to stay inside while he unhooked the trailer. He pulled it close to the trail that led to the cave and parked.

As Vicki and the others said one last good-bye, Pete hurried inside. His face was pale.

"What is it?" Conrad said.

Pete pointed toward the highway. Exiting the ramp and heading straight for the gas station was a white GC van.

※

Judd urged Nada to phone her parents and explain what they had discovered about Kasim. Her mother and father were still upset with her but glad to hear the news.

Judd arranged to take Nada back to Kweesa's apartment but didn't tell her about Pavel's hunch. He didn't want to upset her.

Judd knew Lionel and Sam were not only upset about Pavel's condition, but also restless. Lionel had thrown out hints about going back to Illinois.

Judd and Nada made it through the tight security and anti-locust gauntlet at the apartment complex. Kweesa met them by the elevators and shook Judd's hand.

Kweesa was tall with long, braided hair. She spoke with a heavy African accent and wore her Global Community uniform. She took them to her apartment and asked about the meeting with Dan Nieters.

Nada told her about the prison. "It was actually pretty disappointing. Dan started ranting and raving about God and they took him away."

Kweesa shook her head. "I've heard those people can act crazy. After all Nicolae Carpathia has done, to say he is anything but God is insanity, right?"

Judd bit his lip. "When the GC found out about Dan, did they go through his apartment?"

Kweesa nodded. "I think they searched it."

"Anything turn up?" Judd said.

"Not that I heard," Kweesa said. "Why?"

"Just a hunch," Judd said. "I figure a guy like that probably wouldn't work alone. Is his apartment still empty?"

"I'm not sure," Kweesa said. She went into another room to find a directory of GC personnel.

"What are you doing?" Nada whispered.

"Just covering the bases," Judd said. "I want to make sure we don't miss any clues."

Kweesa returned, flipping through the directory. "Here it is. He lived in this building, only three floors below me."

✳

Vicki froze. They were so close to leaving and now this.

"Let's get out of here," Conrad said.

Pete shook his head. "They'll nab us for sure. Better play it cool."

The kids split up and sat in different booths in the diner. Pete hid in the office and let Roger answer the GC's questions. Instead of refueling, the van parked so it blocked the front door.

This doesn't look good, Vicki thought.

Locusts swarmed around the van. A man in white protective gear got out of the driver's side and carefully stepped inside the station.

Vicki sat at the last booth, her back to the door. The man squeezed through the door without letting any locusts in.

"What can I do for you?" Roger said from behind the counter.

The man spoke through a speaker inside the helmet. "Are there any GC Peacekeepers here?"

"Looks like you're the only one, pal," Roger said. "You and whoever's in that van out front."

"I'm alone," the man said. "I'm looking for somebody."

"OK," Roger said. "Can't say I know everybody around here. Who are you looking for?"

"Followers of Tsion Ben-Judah," the Peace-keeper said. "I'm looking for believers in Jesus Christ."

⁜

Judd said good-bye to Nada and Kweesa and took the stairs three floors down. Dan's apartment was at the end of a hallway. He approached carefully, trying not to make noise.

Judd found the apartment and stood outside. Even if someone new lived there now, Dan might have left a clue about Kasim the GC had overlooked. A couple dressed in GC uniforms opened a door behind him.

The man looked at Judd. "Can I help you?"

"Somebody told me this was the place where Dan Nieters lived," Judd said.

"It was," the man said. "You a friend?"

"Don't know the guy," Judd said, "just heard he was one of those religious fanatics."

"Yeah," the man said, "a shame too. Dan was a hard worker. He could have done a lot of good if he hadn't been brainwashed."

"Does anybody live here now?" Judd said.

"Haven't assigned it yet." The man squinted at Judd. "How did you get in here?"

Judd cleared his throat. "I dropped off a friend upstairs. Just thought I'd stop and see where the crazy guy lived."

Judd was glad when the man and his wife turned to leave. *I'd better get out of here fast.* The woman glanced at him and Judd turned back to Dan's apartment. What he saw took his breath away. The peephole in the apartment was dark. When Judd turned, it was light again.

Someone's in Dan's apartment! Judd thought.

⁂

Vicki gasped. She glanced back just as the Peacekeeper unlatched his helmet. Oxygen hissed as it escaped the airtight suit.

"You're looking for those crazy people who think God's behind all that's happening?" Roger said.

The man nodded and took off his helmet. On his forehead was the mark of the true believer.

"I don't believe it!" Roger said. "You're one of us."

The man smiled. Pete came out from the office and called the others. The man in the white suit shook hands and hugged everyone. "I sure am glad to see some of my own kind."

"You don't know how glad we are to see you," Pete said, introducing himself. "We've been hiding out since those two Peacekeepers got stung."

"So you're the one who was driving the truck?" the man said.

"You bet," Pete said, putting an arm around Vicki. "Me and my little accomplice, Vicki."

The man smiled at Vicki and put out a hand. "Pleased to meet you, Vicki. I'm Chris Traickin."

ELEVEN

Taking Chances

"YOU'RE the former senator!" Vicki said. "We tried to warn you about the GC, but we got stuck here."

"I heard on the news that you escaped," Pete said. "How did you do it?"

Chris Traickin shook his head. "Everybody talks about the Global Community having the best and brightest, but I don't see it. Two Peacekeepers were transferring me and I knocked them both out. I changed into this outfit and took the van."

"How did you know to come here?" Conrad said.

"I heard the GC talking about a group of Ben-Judah followers in this area," Traickin said. "I listened to the radio and followed their signals. Finding you guys was just blind luck."

Conrad checked out the GC suit. "What happened to your friends in Baltimore?"

Traickin pursed his lips. "We were headed for a meeting. I stopped at my apartment and heard a phone message from someone saying I'd better get out of there."

"That was Mark!" Shelly said. "He's back in Illinois at the school—"

Conrad interrupted. "If you knew the GC was going to crack down, how did you get caught?"

"I rushed to the meeting to warn my friends," Traickin said. "Before I could get everybody out, the GC showed up in full force."

Traickin explained that the GC had separated him from the others when they recognized who he was. "They took me to a different jail to question me."

"What are you going to do now?" Pete said.

Traickin frowned. "Hadn't really planned anything more than finding some other believers and trying to stay away from the GC. I guess I'm on their most-wanted list now."

Conrad muttered something. While Pete and Roger talked more with Traickin, Vicki pulled Conrad aside. "What's the matter with you? Why are you being so cold?"

Conrad leaned close to Vicki and whispered, "Something's not right with this guy."

"Are you kidding?" Vicki said. "He's a hero."

"I don't know," Conrad said. "The way he got away from the GC, the fact that he has one of their vans and they haven't found him, the way he said luck brought him to us. How did he know Pete drove the truck?"

"He probably heard it on the radio," Vicki said. She couldn't believe Conrad was so suspicious of their new friend. "What about the mark on his forehead?"

Conrad shook his head. "I don't know."

Vicki rolled her eyes. "I don't believe this. If he's not one of us, why hasn't he been stung by a locust?"

"How long you think he's had that suit on?" Conrad said.

Vicki walked away. Conrad called after her but she joined the others.

"It's settled," Pete said.

"What's settled?" Vicki said.

Pete put his arm around Traickin. "We're taking our friend back with us to Illinois."

※

Judd met with Lionel and Sam when he returned to Pavel's apartment. They hadn't heard from Mr. Rudja about Pavel's condition.

Lionel shook his head when Judd told him about the mysterious person in Dan's apartment. "You're lucky you got out of there without being arrested."

"You think it was GC?" Judd said.

"Who else?" Lionel said. "They've probably planted somebody to watch the place."

Sam cleared his throat. "I know we're waiting on news from Pavel, but do you have any idea when we're leaving?"

Judd looked at Lionel.

"We've been talking," Lionel said. "I don't think it's good for Sam to go back to Israel. I want to take him to the schoolhouse."

"That's a long way from home," Judd said to Sam.

"When I became a believer in Christ, my home changed," Sam said. "It's been wonderful being with other believers. I've studied and learned a lot from Lionel since we've been here. But the longer we stay, the more anxious I am to leave New Babylon."

"Me too," Lionel said. "I don't know what that means for you and Nada."

Judd put his head in his hands. He knew he had to make a decision soon. Would he start a new life with Nada or return to the States?

Before he could speak, the phone rang. It was Mr. Rudja at the hospital.

"How is he?" Judd said.

Pavel's father could hardly speak. At last he whispered, "My son is finally free of pain. He is with his mother now. And he is with God."

※

If Conrad hadn't told her his suspicions, Vicki would have been elated. Transporting Chris Traickin to Illinois and helping him escape the GC would encourage all believers. But Vicki couldn't get Conrad's words out of her mind. She stared at the mark on Traickin's forehead. Was it her imagination or was there something strange about it? And there seemed to be more locusts swarming around the windows of the gas station since he had arrived.

Vicki wanted to talk with Pete, but the more she thought, the sillier she felt. What would she do, ask to inspect the former senator's mark? Open the door and ask him to run around outside without protective clothing?

Pete suggested they get rid of the GC van. Roger knew about an old barn a few miles into the hills where they could stash it. "Who knows, the thing might come in handy one of these days," Roger said.

While Roger drove the van away, Pete and the others waited.

Conrad whispered to Vicki, "I'm going to expose this guy."

Judd phoned Nada with the news of Pavel's death. She wept and asked to meet with him. "Kweesa isn't here, and I don't want to be alone."

"I understand," Judd said. He suggested they meet outside the GC building so Judd wouldn't have to go through security.

Lionel spoke up. "You think we should get out of here soon?"

"Mr Rudja can arrange for us to stay," Judd said. "Let's wait until after the funeral and figure out our next move."

Lionel hesitated.

"What?" Judd said.

"I've been checking possible flights," Lionel said. "Chloe Williams gave me the names of some pilots who have signed on with the believers' co-op."

"What are you saying?" Judd said.

"If I can arrange a flight back to the States, I'm going ahead. You can come if you want."

Judd felt his face flush with anger. "Can't you wait until we bury my friend? Don't you even care?"

Lionel sighed. "I know this is a rough time to bring it up. This may be our best shot."

"Fine," Judd said. "Make your plans."

Judd briskly walked into a beautiful New Babylon sunset. The buildings glistened with light. The sight was stunning. But with the death of his friend and an uncertain future, it was more than he could bear. Judd stopped and tears rolled down his cheeks.

He met Nada at the corner of the building and they walked across a plaza and found a bench behind a row of shrubs. Nada put her head on Judd's shoulder. "I'm so sorry."

"It's just beginning to sink in," Judd said. "I know he's in a better place, but it went so fast."

"You can be happy you were part of the reason he's in such a good place," Nada said. "You were the one who told him about God."

"It was one of the best things that's happened to me since the vanishings," Judd said.

As they sat together, Judd spilled everything. He told her Lionel's plan to return to Illinois with Sam, Pavel's words to Judd the last time he had seen him, and what Judd had seen outside Dan Nieters' door.

Nada pulled away. "We have to go to Dan's apartment."

"Lionel thinks it's a trap," Judd said.

"Perhaps," Nada said. "But maybe someone's there who knew Kasim. We could find out for sure about his decision."

Judd tried to talk her out of it, but Nada said she would go alone if he didn't come with her.

"All right," Judd said, "let's go."

🌟

Vicki grabbed Conrad's arm. "What are you going to do?"

"Watch," Conrad said.

Vicki followed him into the office. Pete was in the middle of a sentence but stopped. "What?"

Conrad looked closely at Traickin's forehead, then stepped back. "I know you used to be a senator, but I've got my doubts about you being one of us."

"Conrad!" Pete shouted.

Chris Traickin held up a hand. "It's OK. I don't blame you for being suspicious."

Pete was enraged. "How can you think . . . ?"

"I have my reasons," Conrad said, "and the first is that mark on your forehead. There's something weird about it."

"Looks the same to me," Pete said, leaning forward.

"What do you see on my forehead?" Conrad said.

The man squinted in the dimly lit room. "The same thing I see on everybody else, a cross."

"When did you first see yours?"

Traickin smiled. "I've never seen my own. Not even in a mirror. But I suppose it looks like yours."

"This will stop right now!" Pete said.

Before Conrad could say anything, Traickin held up a hand. "You're probably wondering about this suit I'm wearing too."

Conrad nodded. "Let's see you take it off and take one step ouside."

"That's enough!" Pete shouted.

Traickin stopped Pete again. "It's a fair question. Two answers. Number one, I think it would be better for all of us if I wear this protective gear."

"So you won't get stung," Conrad said.

"No, in case we get stopped by the GC," Traickin said, "I might be able to bluff my way around them in this costume."

"What's the second reason?" Conrad said.

"It's kind of embarrassing," Traickin said.

"Humor me."

Traickin smiled. "Ever since I was a kid, I've had this fear of bugs. Maybe a spider crawled on me when I was little, I don't know. When I first got a look at those locusts, I was terrified. Even though I'm a believer, even though I'm an adult, I'm scared. I've stayed inside most of the time. I just can't stand the thought of having one of those things touch me."

Conrad stared at the man. After an awkward silence, Traickin sighed. He unsnapped and unzipped his protective suit.

"What are you doing?" Pete said.

"It's obvious there's only one way to prove I'm the real thing. I'm going to take this off and head outside for a little chat with those slimy—"

"No, you're not," Pete said. "This is ridiculous. You're one of us and that's that."

Conrad turned away. Traickin put a hand on his shoulder. "Look at me."

Conrad turned.

"I believe in God," Traickin said. "My wife disappeared and I searched for answers. I found them on Tsion Ben-Judah's Web site. I asked God to forgive me and I gave him my life."

Pete stood and hugged the man. "That's enough for me." He looked at Conrad. "Are you satisfied?"

Conrad glanced at Traickin, then walked away.

Traickin looked at Vicki. "You believe me, don't you?"

Vicki smiled. "Of course. Conrad's been through a lot."

Pete grabbed more supplies and headed for the truck. "We'll leave as soon as Roger gets back."

※

Judd and Nada rode the elevator and found Dan Nieters' apartment. They stood in the shadows by a stairwell and waited.

"Maybe I could get some tools and we could pick the lock," Nada suggested.

"They'll hear us. Does Kweesa have an extra uniform?"

"A bunch."

"What if we find something to deliver? A letter or a package?"

"And I could dress as a GC worker and get a look at whoever's in there," Nada interrupted.

"I was thinking I would go."

Nada smirked. "You wouldn't look good in her uniform."

Judd watched the hallway while Nada went to Kweesa's room to change. She returned a few minutes later with a small package under her arm. "How do I look?"

"Pants are a little long, but I'd hire you," Judd said. "What's in the package?"

"One of the GC handbooks autographed by Nicolae Carpathia himself."

"You're kidding!" Judd said.

Nada smirked again. "Just signing the name made me feel powerful."

"I'll wait here," Judd said. "Promise you'll do what we agreed. Put the package on the floor, knock, and get out of there."

"Why are we doing this if I can't talk with them about my brother?" Nada said.

"Let's see who opens the door. And remember to put the package in the hall so the person has to step out to get it."

Nada kissed Judd on the cheek. "Just let us Global Community workers do our job, OK?"

Nada straightened her uniform and walked down the corridor. She slowed when she came to the apartment and put her ear to the door.

Come on, Judd thought, *just knock and get out of there.*

Nada placed the package on the floor a couple of feet from the door.

Good job.

Nada knocked lightly and put her eye to the peephole.

"Nada," Judd whispered, "get out of there!"

She put a finger to her lips and pointed

toward the door. "I think somebody's coming."

Judd's heart beat faster. The elevator dinged. A man and woman got off the elevator and headed down another corridor.

A lock clicked. Judd glanced at Nada. She picked up the package as the door opened. "Someone at the front asked me to deliver this," Nada said.

Her voice trailed as she straightened and looked at the person. Judd strained to see but couldn't.

Suddenly, Nada cried out and crumpled to the floor. Judd rushed to her. A man stepped out and said, "Help me get her inside."

Judd dropped to the floor to help Nada but she was out cold. He stole a glance to see what had shocked her. Judd couldn't believe his eyes.

ABOUT THE AUTHORS

Jerry B. Jenkins (www.jerryjenkins.com) is the writer of the Left Behind series. He owns the Jerry B. Jenkins Christian Writers Guild, an organization dedicated to mentoring aspiring authors. Former vice president for publishing for the Moody Bible Institute of Chicago, he also served many years as editor of *Moody* magazine and is now Moody's writer-at-large.

His writing has appeared in publications as varied as *Reader's Digest, Parade, Guideposts,* in-flight magazines, and dozens of other periodicals. Jenkins's biographies include books with Billy Graham, Hank Aaron, Bill Gaither, Luis Palau, Walter Payton, Orel Hershiser, and Nolan Ryan, among many others. His books appear regularly on the *New York Times, USA Today, Wall Street Journal,* and *Publishers Weekly* best-seller lists.

Jerry is also the writer of the nationally syndicated sports story comic strip *Gil Thorp,* distributed to newspapers across the United States by Tribune Media Services.

Jerry and his wife, Dianna, live in Colorado and have three grown sons.

Dr. Tim LaHaye (www.timlahaye.com), who conceived the idea of fictionalizing an account of the Rapture and the Tribulation, is a noted author, minister, and nationally recognized speaker on Bible prophecy. Dr. LaHaye was chosen the "Most Influential Evangelical of the Last Twenty-Five Years" by the Institute for the Study of American Evangelicals at Wheaton College. He is the founder of both Tim LaHaye Ministries and The PreTrib Research Center. He also recently cofounded the Tim LaHaye School of Prophecy at Liberty University. Presently Dr. LaHaye speaks at many of the major Bible prophecy conferences in the U.S. and Canada, where his current prophecy books are very popular.

Dr. LaHaye holds a doctor of ministry degree from Western Theological Seminary and a doctor of literature degree from Liberty University. For twenty-five years he pastored one of the nation's outstanding churches in San Diego, which grew to three locations. It was during that time that he founded two accredited Christian high schools, a Christian school system of ten schools, and Christian Heritage College.

Dr. LaHaye has written over forty books that have been published in more than thirty languages. He has written books on a wide variety of subjects, such as family life, temperaments, and Bible prophecy. His current fiction works, the Left Behind series, written with Jerry B. Jenkins, continue to appear on the bestseller lists of the Christian Booksellers Association, *Publishers Weekly*, *Wall Street Journal*, *USA Today*, and the *New York Times*.

He is the father of four grown children and grandfather of nine. Snow skiing, waterskiing, motorcycling, golfing, vacationing with family, and jogging are among his leisure activities.

The Future Is Clear

Check out the exciting Left Behind: The Kids series

BOOKS #23 AND #24 COMING SOON!